I Didn't Say Goodbye

CLAUDINE VEGH

I Didn't Say Goodbye

with an Afterword
by Bruno Bettelheim

Translated by Ros Schwartz

E. P. DUTTON, INC.   NEW YORK

Published in the United States by E. P. Dutton, Inc.
2 Park Avenue, New York, N.Y. 10016

Library of Congress Catalog Card Number: 84-73047

ISBN: 0-525-24308-9

Published simultaneously in Canada by Fitzhenry & Whiteside Limited,
Toronto

10 9 8 7 6 5 4 3 2 1

COBE

To live, as well as to die,
a Jewish father needs to know
that the future of his child
is secure.

Sigmund Freud

For my children
ERIC and MAGALI

List of Contents

LANDMARKS

1940

10 June	THE GERMANS INVADE FRANCE
25 June	Franco-German armistice. France is divided into two zones.
	The Germans occupy the northern zone. Pétain sets up his government in Vichy, in the southern zone, called the "unoccupied" or "free" zone.
10 July	Pétain becomes the French "Head of State" and Prime Minister. Deputy Prime Minister, Pierre Laval.
July-August	"Doriotist" (see p.145) action groups attack shops owned by Jews, provocation intended to make the measures taken by the Germans appear necessary.
15 July	First German order concerning works of art and documents belonging to Jews.
16 July	Jews of Alsace and Lorraine sent to the unoccupied zone.
17 July	Promulgation of law restricting civil-servants, aimed at the Jews in particular.
22 July	Revision of naturalization granted after August 1927.
23 July	The Vichy law providing for the selling off of Jewish-owned property to go to the Secours National Français is refused by the

	Germans, who want to keep their rights over this property.
19-30 August	The Germans forbid the Jews who fled the invasion to return to the occupied zone and announce that a census will be taken.
27 Aug.	Abrogation of the Marchandeau law of 21 April 1939 which punished excesses of the press in racial or religious matters.
27 September	A German order provides for a census of Jews and their property to be carried out. The copy of the original filing card, compiled by local police stations, is passed on to the Gestapo.
October	Jews in the occupied zone are ordered to report to the police and to have "JEW" stamped on their identity cards.
3 Oct.	Vichy promulgates the "Jews' Statute": the Jews, (except for war veterans) are to be excluded from high positions, (administrative, judicial, police, military, teaching. . .) They are not allowed to hold posts of responsibility in the press, radio, cinema etc. Anyone who has three Jewish grandparents, or a Jewish spouse and two Jewish grandparents, will be considered a Jew.
4 Oct.	A law authorising Prefects to intern foreign Jews in special camps, or to place them under house-arrest (amongst these Jews are those who lost their citizenship on 22 July.)
7 Oct.	Algerian Jews deprived of French nationality, granted by the Crémieux Decree in 1870.
18 Oct.	Administrators nominated to take over Jewish firms.
24 Oct.	Meeting between Pétain and Hitler in Montoire: the principle of Franco-German collaboration is adopted.

1941

29 March	The Vichy government sets up the *Commissariat Général aux Questions Juives* (a commission to deal with Jewish affairs). Xavier Vallat is the Commissioner.
26 April	In the occupied zone the Jews are banned from economic activities. The administrators nominated in Jewish firms are authorised to sell off to anybody who is Aryan, or to liquidate the company.
11 May	The S.S. Commander Dannecker, Eichmann's subordinate in France, founds the Institute of Jewish Studies, and its annexe, The Friends of the Institute, which organizes demonstrations, anti-Jewish propaganda etc.
13 May	Hundreds of police officers send summonses to the Jews living in Paris, later called the "green card".
14 May	Thousands of foreign Jews arrested by the French police and imprisoned at Beaune-la-Rolande, and Pithiviers. Then a succession of round-ups in the occupied zone.
2 June	Law of 2 June: All Jews are excluded from managerial posts. In private enterprise, they are excluded from numerous activities. Census extended to the unoccupied zone. It is compulsory to have "JEW" stamped on identity cards and ration books.
22 June	GERMAN OFFENSIVE AGAINST U.S.S.R.
11 August	Numerus clausus (previously instigated for lawyers) extended to doctors, universities, even to schools, in Algeria.
12 Aug.	Round-up in Paris, coinciding with the opening of the camp at Drancy.
13 Aug.	In the occupied zone confiscation of wireless

	sets belonging to Jews, then of bicycles. The Post Office is ordered to cut off phones belonging to Jews.
20 Aug.	First internal ruling that makes Drancy a military prison, (under French administration).
21 Aug.	Round-up in the 11th district in Paris. All Jewish lawyers living in Paris are interned.
Night of 2/3 October	Six Synagogues blown up in Paris by the fascist group Deloncle.
November	Vichy sets up the *Police pour Questions Juives*. First convoys of Jews from eastern Europe arrive at Auschwitz.
29 Nov.	At the request of the German Embassy and of the Gestapo, Xavier Vallat, Commissioner for Jewish Affairs, creates the *Union Générale des Israelites de France* (U.G.I.F.) The purpose of this Union is to enclose the Jews. There are similar organizations in Germany and Poland. It encompasses existing Jewish institutions.
7 December	THE UNITED STATES OF AMERICA ENTERS THE WAR The Paris police H.Q. issues an order forbidding Jews to change their residence – restriction of movement.
12 Dec.	1000 Jews, mainly French, intellectuals and people of influence, are arrested in Paris. They are to be deported to Auschwitz in 1942.
1942 20 January	The conference of Wannsee Strasse, in Berlin, rules the "final solution" to the Jewish problem. They decide to exterminate the Jews of Europe. The Germans obtain the participation of the French police for the first deportation operations.

7 February	German ruling forbids Jews in the occupied zone to leave their homes between 8 p.m. and 6 a.m.
27 March	First deportation of French Jews: 1000 eminent people, arrested in December 1941 sent to the death camps.
April	Pierre Laval, having taken a back seat for a while, comes back to the Vichy cabinet with increased powers. He reinforces the policy of collaboration with Germany.
6 May	X. Vallat, considered too moderate, hands over to Darquier de Pellepoix at the *Commissariat Général aux Questions Juives.*
29 May	A ruling makes it compulsory for Jews over the age of six to wear the yellow star "firmly sewn on to their clothes."
1 July	Eichmann comes to Paris to confer with Dannecker. He recommends increasing the rate of deportation, which is, at that point, 3000 Jews a week, 3 convoys of 1000 people, departure from Drancy.
3 July	Arrest of patients interned at the Rothschild Hospital in Paris. Pierre Laval suggests the deportation of Jewish children aged under 16 from the unoccupied zone.
5 July	Darquier de Pellepoix sets up the Enquiry and Control Dept. to replace the Police for Jewish Affairs (banned because of a scandal). Their job is to report "delinquents" to an anti-Jewish section. People requested to inform on and denounce Jews.
8 July	In the occupied zone Jews banned from theatres, restaurants, public parks etc. They will be allowed to do their shopping between 3 and 4 p.m. A fine of 1 million francs must be paid by the

	Jews, following an attack committed against the Germans in Paris (raised by the U.G.I.F.)
16-17 July	The *Vél d'hiv* raid. The French police organize and execute the rounding up of 12,284 Jews in Paris. They are confined in the *Vélodrome d'Hiver*, rue Nélation, before being taken to Drancy, Beaune-la-Rolande and Pithiviers, and finally deported on 21 July. For the first time, women and children are also arrested.
Summer	Efforts to save the children are multiplied. Convoys are organized to convey them to hiding places in France, or across to Switzerland.
10 August	In the unoccupied zone Jews who arrived in France after 1936 are rounded up. The Vichy Government hands over 15,000 foreign Jews to the Germans.
23 September	In the weekly '*Je Suis Partout*' (I Am Everywhere) the writer Robert Brasillach attacks those who (like the Archbishop of Toulouse) protest against the brutality and the separation: "that all of us are prepared to disapprove of, as it is necessary to separate the Jews as a whole, and not keep the children."
8 November	ALLIED FORCES LAND IN NORTH AFRICA
11 Nov.	Total occupation of France by the Germans and Italians, (the latter East of the Rhône). Arrest and deportation of French and foreign Jews.
11 December	Law making it compulsory for Jews all over France to have "JEW" stamped on their identity cards and ration books.
20 Dec.	The Prefect of the Alpes Maritimes decides to deport all foreign Jews. The Italians try to oppose this and are prepared to take

	control of the Jews. The Jews leave Nice, but many of them are arrested.
1943	Henceforth the Germans and the police H.Q. rehouse French and German people in the flats "abandoned" by the Jews.
30 January	Pétain and Laval found the French Militia, the Head of which is Joseph Darnand. A political, police and military organization, the Militia fight against the Resistance but also engage in the rounding up of Jews.
25 February	MUSSOLINI FALLS.
April-May	The Jewish Army (to become the *Organisation Juive de Combat*) is set up in the Tarn region maquis (Resistance).
2 July	Drancy turned over to German administration.
August	Jewish scout organization puts itself under the orders of the O.J.C.
8 September	GERMANS CONTROL ALL ITALIAN RAILWAY SERVICES. ITALY CAPITULATES. THE ITALIAN ZONE (S.E. FRANCE) IS OCCUPIED BY THE GERMANS. Numerous round-ups organized.
31 December	Darnand, Chief of the Militia, becomes National Chief of Police.
1944	
15, 18, 24 March	Jewish refugees in Monaco rounded up. (Monaco had remained neutral until then).
6 April	Germans seize the children at the Izieu Home near Lyon and deport them.
6 June	ALLIED FORCES LAND IN NORMANDY
13 Aug.	Railway workers protest strike.
15 Aug.	FRENCH AND ALLIED TROOPS LAND IN PROVENCE.
17 Aug.	Germans abandon Drancy after last convoy

	has left.
19 August	Pithiviers camp is liberated.
25 Aug.	PARIS IS LIBERATED
26 November	Himmler has the gas chambers in the concentration camps destroyed so that no proof remains.

1945

8 May	SIGNING OF THE ARMISTICE
April-May	The survivors of the concentration camps return: they are welcomed at the Hotel Lutetia in Paris. Out of 75,721* people deported from France, only 2,500 came back.

*Minimum figure given by S. & B. Klarsfeld: *Le Memorial de la Déportation des Juifs de France*, Paris 1978.

I DIDN'T SAY GOODBYE

Introduction

Why these interviews? Originally they were for a dissertation I was to submit to the University to conclude my studies in Psychiatry.

I had been working for more than six months on a completely different topic, and then, one Sunday morning, at the little Synagogue in the Paris suburb of Aulnay-sous-Bois, one of my daughter's friends, Maurice, had his *Bar Mitzvah*.

From the beginning of the ceremony, his mother covered her face with her hands and remained tense and withdrawn. Maurice sang fervently without taking his eyes off his mother who was sobbing... eyes which held a mixture of incomprehension and terrible sadness.

Sitting next to me was a woman of Tunisian origin who kept repeating: "I don't understand... on this occasion a mother is so proud of her son, so happy... what's going on? This is a holiday!"

But I could understand. A year ago, in that same Synagogue, my son had put on the *Tallith*,* reviving the painful memory of my own father. I had not experienced my son's *Bar Mitzvah* as a joyful occasion either: it was, rather, a painful link with the past, a kind of torch which my son was receiving in his turn.

It is very difficult to be a Jew; to insist on remaining one, when one is, as I am, neither practising nor even a believer,

*Prayer shawl worn by men

may seem aberrant. But to refuse one's Jewishness would somehow be unbearable. The fact that my two children decided of their own accord to have a *Bar Mitzvah* eased a wound deep inside me. I do not really know in what way.

That morning I felt I had to unveil the past of those Jewish children who survived, and who have been wondering for thirty years why they are alive and by what miracle. Having escaped persecution by the Nazis, I have always had the impression that life has been "granted" to me a second time.

And so I had to show that I deserved that life, that I was worthy to live it. It was no longer even mine; I was living, in a way, by proxy.

In 1942 my parents and I took refuge in a village in the Pyrenees where there was already another Jewish family, from Belgium. The youngest of their children, Régine, was my friend. Very early one morning, the French police came for them; her mother had collected some of their belongings together; a motor-coach was waiting for them.

As they passed our house, Régine asked the driver if he would stop for five minutes so that she could say goodbye to me. He stopped the coach and she came into the house. I remember my father went out, thinking that if the driver had stopped to let Régine come in, perhaps he would agree to leave without her? It was her mother who stopped him. It would be too complicated, she said. Régine had never been away from her family. The coach left; the whole family was deported. Nobody returned.

After the War we read an advertisement in a Jewish newspaper; a relative had published a photograph of the family, asking anyone who recognized one of its members to get in touch with him. My mother wrote to him and he insisted on coming from Belgium to talk about them.

The day that Régine was taken away, my parents decided to leave the village; perhaps we would not be spotted so quickly in a larger town? We arrived in Saint-Girons, in the Ariège region.

My father was torn between two apartments; he chose the second one as the neighbour who had shown him round seemed to be a "good person", he said. Later events proved him right; the same neighbour and her husband became my "godparents", and it is they who hid me for more than two years.

One morning, some French police inspectors came to warn my parents that they would be coming back to take us to a special residence... and so, "godfather", who was the manager of the Credit Lyonnais Bank, had one of their trailers brought over which he attached to the bicycle. In less than half an hour, my parents were hidden inside. When it was time for me to get in, there was not much room and "godmother" suddenly suggested: "Why not leave the child with us? She will only be a burden to you. We have no children; she'll be our daughter, our pride and joy, trust us."

I was trembling with fear. I only wanted them to hurry up and leave so that they would not be arrested. I said: "Go quickly, go quickly, I'm staying." I often heard my "godparents" say I was a gift from God: that is how important I was to them. My parents reached Toulouse and then the region of Grenoble. I wrote to them every day. It was my own decision to do so. Did they receive all my letters? I have no idea. A short time after their departure, they managed to send me a false identity card, but I refused to change my name. I was called Claudine Rozengard and I did not want to be Christine I-don't-know-what.

I was so stubborn that, in spite of all my "godparents'" explanations and exhortations, I still refused. "Godmother" suggested that I adopt their name: Caperan; "godfather" had a niece, they would try to find a way... I refused even more vehemently; I can still picture them, it was quite beyond their understanding: "She is usually so reasonable", they kept saying.

I wanted to keep my name. I was very much afraid that my parents would not be able to find me again. I would grow, change; and supposing they would not be able to recognize me?

One incident has stayed in my mind; I was a bright pupil at school; prize-day was drawing near. My "godparents" were bursting with pride at the thought of the prize I was going to receive. Then a letter arrived from my father, instructing me not to attend the prize-giving ceremony. I was to report sick beforehand, so that my name would not be read out and repeated; it was too dangerous. When my "godparents" read the letter, it was too much for them. "Godfather" had been waiting for this day all year, and "godmother" was planning to dress up for the occasion. I had to go; I could not do that to them.

As for me, I wanted to go on to the platform and receive my prize books; and so I went. Every time my name was spoken I looked round the room like a hunted animal, expecting to be arrested at once. Nothing of the sort happened. The following year, I was at the bottom of my class; the problem did not arise.

For the oral part of my matriculation examination, the last test was Geography. Before I began, the teacher told me in a triumphant voice that I only needed two more marks to gain a distinction; it was virtually in the bag. Then, suddenly, I asked him to give me a naught for that test. As I knew that I had passed my matriculation, I did not want to go on with it.

He suggested that I have a little rest, he tried to understand what was going on; I retorted obstinately:

"Please give me a naught, I cannot go on any longer."

"You must be very tired, I am only going to ask you a very simple question; it will be impossible to give a wrong answer. What is the name of the river that flows through Lyon? Look, I know you know the answer; I will help you: the Rh... the Rh..."

And I answered: "The Rhine, which separates us from Germany."

I was not awarded a "distinction"; he was shattered; I was relieved; neither he nor I understood what had happened.

Subsequently, I refused to take any competitive examinations. It took me years to understand the significance of that decision.

In 1943 my parents made preparations to cross to Switzerland. They phoned to let "godfather" know, and asked him to take me to a certain town. "Godfather" and "godmother" refused to let me leave, they said they didn't want to give me back to my parents. "Besides, it's too dangerous," they added, "here, at least you are safe." But, as I refused to stay, and because I begged them to take me there, they added: "If your parents abandon you again, there won't be anyone to take you in, we're warning you, we won't be able to take you back."

Had my parents "abandoned" me? It wasn't possible, it wasn't true! But, after all, they had gone away and left me with strangers, so... My parents did not want to leave for Switzerland without me. At that time, any Jewish child could be arrested. I, however, was not worried.

The whole town of Saint-Girons knew that I was a little Jewish girl that Mr and Mrs Caperan were looking after, their adopted daughter: "the poor things, they had so desperately wanted a child", people would say. When I had a teacher whose husband was a pro-German sympathizer, I stopped going to school; then she was replaced and I went back.

The headmaster had assured "godfather" that if the Germans raided the school, he would be the first to hear about it, and, as he lived on the premises, there was nothing to be afraid of.

As for "godmother", one day she went to see the leader of the Militia (they had been very good friends before the War) and asked him to protect me. "I want you to know that if they touch a hair of that child's head, I'm the one who'll die." I was in the room during that conversation; she cried, he reassured her and promised that nobody would harm me.

After France was liberated, each day I awaited my parents' return. I would picture it: one day I'd come home from school and they would be waiting for me. I could hear the laughter, I could imagine the hugs and even the presents they would bring. The reality was not quite like that.

Effectively, one day, on my way home from school, a neighbour said to me: "Claudine, hurry, there's a surprise waiting for you." I flung down my satchel, I said: "It's my parents!" and rushed off.

"Wait!" she then shouted, "your mother's there but your father's dead..."

I stopped in my tracks, I picked up my satchel, I climbed the stairs that led to the flat, went towards my mother, and without shedding a tear, I simply said to her: "I've heard... at least I've got one of you, let's never talk about it again."

And, for more than twenty years, I was never able to pronounce the words "daddy" or "father", nor could I bear to hear any allusion to that period of my childhood.

Mummy wanted to take me back, "godfather" and "godmother" wanted to keep me. As for me, I wanted to go and live with my mother. I hadn't seen her for more than two years; yes, I had been very happy with "godfather" and "godmother", but I wanted to go home.

"Godmother" thought I was just ungrateful; she should have thought ahead; she regretted allowing herself to get so fond of me; it was certain, they would both die of sorrow, and it would be my fault.

"Godfather" died three years after I went back to Paris. "Godmother" said to anyone who would listen: "After the child left he lost the will to live, it killed him."

I found it very difficult to cope with the situation. I spent all my holidays with them; a week before I was due to leave for Paris I would watch them grow sad, I suffered from this immensely but I forced myself not to show my feelings. The Stationmaster told me, many years later, that two or three days before I arrived, "godfather" would make his way to the station, on foot, to watch the train that would soon be bringing me.

For me, all that was heart-rending, I felt literally torn. My debt was very heavy, too heavy.

After "godfather's" death, Mummy invited "godmother" to come and live with us; she accepted immediately. She, who had never left the countryside, ended up in Paris, and has lived there ever since.

Not long ago, a friend said to her, "You love Claudine as a daughter," and "godmother", now aged eighty-six, replied indignantly, "But it's not *as*, she *is* my daughter. Nobody

understands, not even you," and she added: "besides, on
Mother's Day, I always get my present..."

"Godmother" and I were both born on Christmas night.
For her this bond held a special significance.

As for my return to Paris, that wasn't easy either. Mummy
had retrieved our old flat; the place was cold, empty and dirty,
too big for the two of us. As soon as she had found a bed, a
kitchen table and two chairs, my mother bought me an old
second-hand piano.

From that day on, my life at home was transformed: when I
came home from school, I was no longer alone in the flat, I had
my piano.

I felt completely lost, even in my daily routine. I was used to
the country, I got lost in the Métro, I got lost in the enormous
building of the Lycée Hélène Boucher; I didn't recognize any
of my relatives, uncles, aunts, cousins; my performance at
school was mediocre, I no longer dared answer in class, as my
southern accent caused general mirth; I told my beads every
evening as "godmother" had taught me, and I sensed that my
mother would have preferred me not to. What is more, my
mother's ideas were completely different from those of my
"godparents" even on matters such as cooking and table
manners.

My paternal grandmother came to live with us at that
point. She only spoke a few words of French. My mother
conversed with her in Yiddish: but I no longer understood a
single word, I had forgotten everything.

I was completely disoriented.

That was when my mother had an idea that she felt ought to
solve my problems: she sensed that I had difficulties re-
adapting, perhaps mixing with other Jewish children who had
similar problems would help me?

So I went to the first summer camp for Jewish children,
organised after the War.

On the first evening, once again I felt at a loss, alone. I didn't
know any of the other children. I shared a room with five other
little girls of my age. I didn't understand; they talked among
themselves, how did they know each other? I asked them if

their parents were friends, if they visited each other in Paris. They looked at me as if I came from outer space, nobody answered. I didn't dare open my mouth again. I felt I had asked an "indecent" question, but no matter how hard I thought about it, I couldn't understand.

The following day, one of the women in charge got wind of my questions and took me aside. She explained that among the children at the camp, there were many who no longer had any parents at all, they all lived together in houses where they were cared for. Such was the case of the five little girls in my room.

It seems I turned so pale that the woman was quite frightened; I remember, I abruptly left the room; I went back to the bedroom, where, fortunately, there was nobody else; I flung myself on the bed, and sobbed my heart out as I had never done before. It was too much for me, I couldn't take any more.

That woman stayed by me for nearly an hour, I refused to let her comfort me, I wanted her to leave me alone.

I was ashamed, I who was lucky enough to still have my mother, I didn't have the right to cry; what was happening to me? And yet I felt desperate.

That same evening, I had a temperature of over 104°. For two days, I ran a high temperature, but had no other symptoms. It seems I was even delirious. But what exactly does 'delirious' mean in that context?

It must be understood that not only were the children traumatised, but the staff who looked after us were also survivors; sometimes we witnessed rather strange incidents: one day, somebody suggested a competition: we were to write a very detailed letter to our parents about the summer-camp; the winning letter would be printed in the *Journal juif* (Jewish newspaper), which was published in Paris! A deathly silence followed this suggestion, it was unbearable, so, I got up and shouted: "I'll do it, I'll write the letter; let's choose another subject for the competition." My letter was published, presented as the winning letter of a competition in which I was the sole entrant!"

What a strange world it was, where the children never spoke of their parents, of their families, of their homes nor of any problem whatsoever!

Laughter, games, dancing, singing, oblivion at all costs or, at least, never to talk "about it", was one of the rules of the camp, a rule that nobody ever enforced! Sadness, a child's grief or tears were felt by everybody, myself included, to be unacceptable.

I never dared tell any of these children that my mother was alive. In any case, nobody would ever have asked; the subject was taboo, absolutely taboo. When I came home from that camp, I had the impression that my life would never again be that of a child; something inside me was shattered; I only realised it at that moment.

I fell ill: a rather particular illness, where the child is subject to fits of uncontrollable shivering. Certain pediatricians maintain that the origin of this illness is psychic. In my case, there is no doubt: for years the symptoms reappeared at the end of October; my father had died in October.

My mother was left a widow at thirty-three. Her life as a woman stopped there. When I asked her to remarry, she replied she had had the good fortune of enjoying twelve years of happiness: "I have enough to live on with my memories", she added.

I was already married when she told me how, as soon as I came back to Paris I worried that my life would be like David Copperfield's. . . She came to the conclusion, in spite of what I said, that the presence of another man would be unwelcome.

Her finest compliment was: "You're the spitting image of your daddy!" I believed her and and I was very proud.

My father had studied law in Warsaw. On the strength of his examination results, the Polish government had awarded him a grant to study for his Ph.D. in Paris. They were reserving the Chair of Criminology at the University of Warsaw for him. To receive a grant, for a Jew, was very rare: to be promised a Chair seemed like a miracle.

On his arrival in France, his only aim was: to live there. He gave up his grant, the Chair, studied for his Ph.D. in

Criminology while preparing for the *Ecole de Sciences Politiques*, and he arranged to bring his whole family over; he was the eldest of seven children.

He fought to have his thesis, *Crime as a Social and Economic Product*, accepted. When he was refused naturalization, one of the reasons put forward was that the content of this research was considered too explosive in 1929.

He would often tell me about his native country: there he had repeatedly suffered humiliation, at school, in everyday life. One day, he rushed up to a Polish officer who had insulted him on purpose, ripped off his epaulettes and trampled on them. If one of his professors had not managed to hush up the affair, he would have been expelled from the University.

He spoke of Poland with bitterness and even with contempt. "How is it possible to live in Poland when one has lived in France?" he would ask. France was the homeland he had chosen, the country of Human Rights, of all freedom and all hope. To breathe did not mean the same thing in Poland as it did in France, and he always ended up saying: "you, who as a child can breathe in this country, never forget how lucky you are!"

He felt profoundly Jewish and, although he had definitely rejected the religious side, Jewish history and the whole Jewish culture remained, in his opinion, extremely important.

He could express himself fluently in five different languages, but anybody could express themselves, he said. What mattered was to study literature, history, tradition, in depth. Culture was to him the most basic need. To describe someone as "a cultured person" was perhaps his highest mark of appreciation.

From 1941 onwards, he was no longer allowed to practise as a lawyer and he spent his time studying, sorting through his documents, making notes, writing; in particular, he was preparing a file on prostitution.

He held conversations with me that one usually has with children much older than I was, but nothing could have been more natural! He wanted me to be able to appreciate the countryside, nature, the smell of the woods, literature, music;

and during our long walks in the Pyrenees he would recite poems by Heine, Schiller, Victor Hugo; he would speak to me of Goethe, Picasso. He was a marvellous whistler, and that is how he familiarized me with the music of Schubert, Bach, Beethoven and Grieg. For a long time, I could not listen to *The Death of Aase* without associating it with my father's death.

What I remember of the years 1941 and 1942 is my father's fierce struggle against the flight of time. Was it because he knew he was seriously ill, or because of the Nazi persecutions?

He spent his time impressing upon me as many things as he could. For my part, I was avid to learn, to listen to him; we got along perfectly.

He taught me the notion of human worth, of moral values. He believed in "humanity", he was an idealist. The idea of justice, the right to live, recurred perpetually. I remember hearing him murmur, on watching a dog: "Why does an animal have the right to live in peace when we don't?"

To keep one's word was sacred; now, he had promised me that he would come back. And for many years, I too refused this "not coming back."

About fifteen years ago, one of my teachers wondered at the fact that "in spite of all they had suffered, Jewish children had come through so well." I remember feeling a certain pleasure at first: we were strong..., and, in the two minutes that followed, a strange mixture of sadness, of anger and even revolt. "It is too easy," I thought, "it is a way of denying all the traumas we have been through or at least of minimising them." And then, after some thought, I came to the conclusion that we, the Jewish children who had lived through the Nazi period, had done all we could to reject that experience as something "outside ourselves".   People who did not suffer bereavement are often reluctant to talk about this period and have a strong desire to dismiss it.

Most of those who were left orphans never talk about their past, it is taboo... they do not want to, above all, they cannot, talk about it.

A friend once said to me: Not to talk about the past is not to blot it out, on the contrary, it is perhaps to try and preserve it in the depths of one's being, like a secret which cannot be shared... the only possible legacy when you have only a blurred image of your parents, and not even a photograph to help retrieve that image."

The same day, by a strange coincidence, he was asked: "Where do you come from?" and I heard him reply ironically, "*Buchenwald*." It is the only allusion to the past he has ever made. Thus one can feel Buchenwaldian... as one can feel French, or Italian... it is simply a way of dealing with one's past!

Only one preoccupation recurred during our conversations: our children's future. Not their professional future, no! But whether they would have the opportunity to get through life without experiencing another genocide?

While there is life there is hope, the saying goes... That is perhaps why we no longer know how to live, because deep down inside, hope... never heard of it.

To carry out these interviews, I asked friends and relatives if they would agree to talk about the war years. Thirty five years later, was it possible for them to talk about "all that"? I specified that it was for a dissertation.

"Was it you who chose a subject like that? What exactly do you want?" I told them: "I don't even know what I myself want."

I was afraid that such an answer might destroy any inclination they might have had to discuss the subject, and I expected a lot of refusals... I only had one, from a psychotherapist whose parents died in deportation.

On the other hand, the question "is there any point in stirring up the past?" did not even arise.

They were all children during the last war. They were all taken away from their families and kept in hiding. They were aged between three and thirteen in 1941, when the persecution began. They are children of people who were deported. With one exception, they themselves were not deported, but they were all left orphans, losing one or both parents. In some cases they are the sole survivors, their whole family having been exterminated in the concentration camps.

I chose to interview people who have all the appearances of being unquestionably integrated, both socially and professionally, people about whom it is said: "They have every reason to be happy".

I let them choose where they were to be interviewed: at home, at my house, at their place of work, in more anonymous surroundings. Only one person chose a café: we were meeting for the first time.

Two preferred to come to my house; all the others asked me to go to their homes, we would have dinner together and then we would "talk about it".

One detail is worth noting: with all the rooms in their flats to choose from, most of them preferred to be interviewed in the bedroom, even though the sitting room was available.

Each interview was conducted in a single session which lasted about two hours. I insisted that they should sit in the place where they felt most at ease, then I sat down close to them.

They all asked me if I was going to record the interview or if I was going to take notes. They expressed their relief when I said I would be content just to listen, but they added that: "if it had been necessary, they would have understood and agreed".

They sat on the edge of their seats, becoming more tense as the interview went on. They shuffled their chairs, overcome with anguish when certain painful moments were evoked. In fact they shifted their position so often that by the end of the session most of them had their backs to me, their gaze riveted on the window...

"The light is too bright in here" is a phrase which often recurred, even though they had ensured from the beginning that we were in semi-darkness.

The interview was, in fact, an endless internal monologue; I was there, but they did not see me. They spoke in a monotone, in a robot-like voice, their faces expressionless, as if they were talking about somebody else... A friend, notorious for his booming voice, expressed himself in a whisper, without even realising he was doing so. As soon as the interview was over, he resumed his normal voice.

At the end of the interview, I asked them why they had
agreed to talk to me.

"To help you."

"So that you could get the material you need."

"I had to go along with you."

"I didn't want to get out of it."

"You needed my co-operation."

"It's like giving blood to a friend."

"Because of the word 'dissertation'."

"Thirty five years afterwards, it's about time... perhaps."

"I needed to talk about it... at least once in my lifetime."

The day after each interview, I telephoned to see how they
were; they felt better, relieved, but I felt progressively worse.
This return to the past was so painful that at one point, I
considered stopping altogether.

A long time elapsed between the actual interview and the
moment when I felt capable of putting it down on paper.

When the dissertation was finished, only three of them
wanted to read it. The others asked me to read certain
fragments aloud to them. It took nearly two years before some
of them acknowledged the existence of their own interviews.

Nobody can imagine what it cost them to "talk about it".

Almost two years will have gone by between the publishing
of the dissertation and that of the book. Most of the people
who read my work asked me to extend it to a wider audience: I
had to go through with it to the end.

The people who took part in the interviews thought for a
long time before agreeing to be thus "stripped" in front of a
completely different public, and I shared their misgivings.

Finally, the general feeling was that the first step had been
taken, but that things should not be allowed to rest there.

LAZARE

I was born in Paris in 1933; my brother in 1935.

I no longer have any distinct memory of my father, only a photograph to cling to.

I think his character was like mine, sometimes sad, taciturn, rather reserved. Quite strict with me; apparently, even then, I was very tough.

You see, I wore the yellow star all the time in Paris. It was terrible. Every recreation, every day after school, the other children would taunt me; I couldn't bear it, I fought to death; I remember my younger brother was in the last year of nursery school, after school he would come and give me a hand. I had to suffer the brutal jokes of my teachers, the clouts. The swine, they took advantage, nobody to stand up for me, they would enjoy themselves at my expense.

Fortunately, I have always been tough. Not one of them made a human gesture, merely human, quite the contrary. Someone would call me a "dirty Jew", I couldn't bear it, I would attack him; they would say that I had started the fight and I would be severely punished for having dared. . . You never forget those things!

It was in '41 that my father left. He received the famous "green card" stipulating that he had to report to the police station otherwise action would be taken against his family.

My father was not stupid. He was not a sheep, but he went to protect us! When they called up young Frenchmen for forced labour in Germany, they went, didn't they? And yet, those men, they already knew. In '41 they believed it was a matter of regrouping Jews in labour camps.

A book has just come out about the "green card", I bought it... I can't bring myself even to open it. It's stupid!

My father was interned in the camp at Pithiviers; he sent us a boat that he had made there, with his own hands, for my brother and me.

My mother started doing odd sewing jobs, we needed money. My mother obtains a permit to visit Pithiviers; she takes us with her. I who am so unruly, I can't make the slightest movement, I remain completely rigid during this visit. My father says adieu, my brother cries, I do not, and all of a sudden my mother utters a howl of pain... she howls to death, I can still hear those cries.

I never saw my father again.

My mother enlists in the Jewish Resistance.

One day she is warned of a raid in our neighbourhood, we lock ourselves in. The police knock at the door, we stand there, all three of us speechless with terror, behind the door, and my mother does not open up. The next day they come back; same setting, we do not open up.

Fortunately the caretaker did not give us away.

For nearly a week we stay locked in like that, with the little food we had. Above all, we were not to make the floorboards creak, or pull the chain, nobody was to know we were there.

Then my mother arranged for us to live with our neighbour on the sixth floor, we lived in her flat for three, four months.

Then, that became too dangerous. My mother put me in the care of the monks near Ménilmontant* and then sent me to stay on a farm with my brother. After six weeks, the farmers wanted to get rid of me, I was a tough nut: so mother found a second family, then a third, a fourth, until... I don't know exactly how many, but, you know, I wasn't happy, as you can imagine. I always had a healthy appetite, I was hungry, and so at night I would go and dig up carrots in the fields and I would scoff them along with anything I could pilfer from the

*A district in the north of Paris.

orchards. I stole at that time, but I stole to survive, I would have done anything.

My mother sometimes came to see us, at night. I knew that she had stayed in Paris, that she worked for the Resistance.

My father had been deported to Auschwitz... I knew that he would not return.

But immediately after France was liberated, every evening, I would listen to the list of survivors... if by good fortune... It was exhausting!

Afterwards, things were difficult. For years, until I earned my own living, we were hard up.

I began high school, I was thirteen; I was the tallest, the strongest and I felt I was the stupidest.

I did not have many friends, I do not make friends easily. I hate new faces.

I can recall one thing; when I came back home, I had acquired lots of strange mannerisms. Then I lost them.

I worked hard. I think my father would have been happy at my success, he would even have been surprised. I had such a difficult nature...

You see, my father answered the summons to protect us, his children, and it is he who... in a way sacrificed himself so that we could live.

I think it is always possible to find a solution; but the one my father found was perhaps not the best; that is all.

I would have done anything to survive, I am a fighter-back, I resist. He must have had his reasons for reporting to the police: The proof is he did protect us. If my mother had not seen what happened to my father she might have opened the door to the police! We almost owe it to him that we are all alive.

I missed my father, I missed my father a lot, but I came through all right, didn't I?

It is in moments of happiness that it is terrible. When I had my viva, I wished he could have been there, or at least seen me.

My sons' *Bar Mitzvahs*. My mother who is a communist and an atheist refused to attend, she even added: "Your father wouldn't have liked this".

To me, it meant retrieving a little of what I had lost... she refuses to understand.

My brother and I both married Catholic women who converted to Judaism without being asked. Our children have all been brought up in the Jewish religion, my grandfather was a Rabbi, you know... And I am involved with a liberal Jewish community.

Six years ago, my car, which was badly parked, was obstructing a neighbour's driveway: I went out to move it, she said "You are just a dirty Jew, what a pity the gas chambers weren't big enough." I managed to keep my temper. I took her to court, she had to move, but I wanted to form a sort of "Jury of Honour" to condemn her in the name of human dignity!

One evening I am called out on an emergency, I forget my identity card, police check. I explain, I tell them who I am, I have a doctor's sticker on my windscreen, I am five minutes from home. "Come with us to the police-station" says the police officer. I had a strange reaction, I said: "Never!" and I lay down in the middle of the road, I refused to move. They carried me to the police-station and it was my wife who brought my documents along and took me home! What is more, whenever I am asked for my identity card I have to control myself, I am subject to terrible fits of anger!

They deducted what I considered an unjustified amount of tax. I never take things lying down: I took them to court, I won. If they had said one word too many I think I would have told them that their fathers had already legally robbed me, were they going to award themselves that same right?

I never talk about the deportation, about the war, about my father. I never go to the cemetery, I can't stand that sort of thing. I went to the Pithiviers memorial ceremony with my mother, and I who am so tough, I completely broke down. I was in such a state... My mother never asked me to go with her again.

It is I who wrote the epitaph which was chosen for the memorial to those who died at Auschwitz.

I only have four children, I should have liked at least six...

Why? Because I would have had two more chances of giving the world, not a genius, but someone who would have been able to help people to live better, and, above all, stop them from exterminating anyone they choose, for any old reason.

I was a fervent communist. I wanted to believe that one day a just and well organised society would exist. When there was the trial of the Jewish doctors in Russia, I left the Party but I never got over it. It was such a great disappointment.

And yet, in my daily life, as soon as something out of the ordinary happens, for example, a relative has an operation, I prepare myself for the worst, I try to face up to all the possibilities imaginable. It's crazy, isn't it? I can't stand it when I hear "You Jews, you're different". But worst of all is when they add "Deep down you don't really consider yourselves French".

After all, perhaps I have become different to the average Frenchman, but whose fault is that? In fact, "they have made me different": I have never forgotten that the police officers who came to get us were French police officers, that my teachers did not once try to shield me from the taunts of the other children, not to mention actively defend me. And people expect me to feel well-adjusted? So what, if I really am different (and that is what frightens them, annoys them) have I not the right to live? To refuse my identity is to refuse my right to live, it's straightforward.

You know, my grandparents, on both sides, died in appalling conditions, the Germans made them dig their own graves first. The aunts and uncles who lived in Poland with my grandparents, two young cousins, they were all exterminated.

From the age of fifteen, sixteen, I did any job I could find, during the holidays and even during term-time, because my mother earned next to nothing, and there was my younger brother. Very early on, instead of being the son, I was the head of the family.

My mother never wanted to remarry or to live with another man. She was left a widow at thirty. My brother and I were everything to her. She totally devoted herself to us.

With a father who died so that we might live, and a mother

who deliberately sacrificed her life as a woman, so as not to impose another man on us, we started out in life already heavily indebted.

***

Lazare, who is endowed with a booming voice, spoke in a whisper throughout this interview.

As soon as the interview was over, his voice resumed its usual tone, he hadn't noticed anything.

On the memorial he had written, in his childlike style:
WE MISS YOU, DARLING DADDY.
ON 14 MAY 1941, THE BOCHE SNATCHED YOU FROM US AND DEPORTED YOU TO PITHIVIERS.
ON 24 JUNE 1942 HITLER'S BRUTES DEPORTED YOU TO AUSCHWITZ.
AND KILLED YOU, AT THE AGE OF THIRTY-FIVE.
WE SHALL NEVER FORGET YOU, DARLING DADDY.
YOU ARE GRAVEN IN OUR MEMORIES FOR EVER.
YOU LEFT TWO CHILDREN. WHEN THEY ARE GROWN UP THEY WILL AVENGE YOU AND HATE THOSE DIRTY HITLERITE VILLAINS.
19 MAY 1946.

ANDRE

My father was a tailor, our income was very modest. At home my parents spoke Yiddish with each other and to me. Before sending me away to boarding school, my mother asked me never to speak another word of Yiddish. I did not ask why, but I was grieved...

We did not have false identity cards. My parents wanted to reach the unoccupied zone. They decided to travel there by coach, but without me.

If they arrived at their destination, they had a trick for getting me there: if they did not arrive, my uncle, who was in the unoccupied zone, would take care of me.

There was an identity inspection on the coach. My father was taken away.

My parents were not able to say goodbye to each other. My mother had had a stroke of luck. She was sitting near a window that was stuck. A police officer was bent on winding it up; he wasted time, became aggravated, and forgot to ask my mother for her papers.

I must add that she has fair hair and blue eyes; but so had my father. In fact, I look very much like my father.

As soon as my mother arrived in the unoccupied zone she paid a neighbour to come and fetch me.

He had a bicycle. I rode on the rack. I remember crossing the demarcation line: for two days he had been drumming into me what I should say if they interrogated me. I was his nephew. I had to call him 'uncle'.

In fact, it was during that journey that I had the feeling something had happened to my father: this neighbour only spoke of my mother, never of my father.

And so I asked more specific questions: "Did my father say that...?" he replied: "Your mother..." etc.

I was agitated. I blamed it all on the war, I was not conscious of being Jewish. I did not wear the star, neither did my parents...

When we crossed the demarcation line, the neighbour left me at the foot of a tree and told me that my uncle, my mother's brother, would come to collect me. Most important, should I be interrogated, I was not to say who had brought me there.

As soon as he left, my uncle arrived. I joined my mother soon after.

"Where's Daddy?"

"The police took him to prison," replied my mother.

"To prison, with thieves? Has Daddy done something wrong?"

I felt lost, I started to cry, I was afraid that my father would be eaten by the rats in prison. My father was very important to me.

My mother and I are living in one room in a house belonging to an old lady. Co-habitation is proving difficult: we move, we find a ground floor flat, we are to stay there until the war is over.

The local people show no animosity towards us, but I feel that I am a stranger to them and that they do not like strangers.

School is a waste of time: I know perfectly well how to read, even so, they put me in the kindergarten; fortunately a teacher settles the problem and subsequently my schooling follows a normal pattern.

I keep my name: and yet I recall one episode: my mother and I take a bus to go and see a very sick aunt. I can still see my mother making me repeat "My name is André Costes..." Fortunately this precaution turned out to be unnecessary.

France is liberated. I wait for my father with total confidence. It never crossed my mind, during all those years, that he would not come back!

And yet we never received a letter from him! In fact I considered him as a prisoner of war, the others were coming back, I was waiting for him.

My mother decides to go back to Paris as quickly as possible, to obtain news of my father. She explains to me that she must go and prepare a place to live and that she would rather I stayed and completed my school year. Some neighbours, whom I know well, have agreed to look after me.

I spend three or four months there; I feel ill at ease in their home, even though they are very kind to me and I am very fond of the eldest son who is seven years my senior. (By the way, I went to visit him a few years ago with my wife and three children: he welcomed us with open arms).

My mother often writes to me; she never mentions my father; I don't understand anything. Why hasn't he come back from Germany yet? In the village where I live, all the prisoners have returned!

My mother comes to fetch me... and then I realise, she comes alone, my father isn't there.

I asked my mother nothing, and, strange as it may seem now, she explained nothing to me.

When I say nothing, I mean nothing. The proof is, when we arrive in Paris, I think we are going back to our old flat: no, we head in a different direction. My mother has not yet been able to get our old flat back; for the time being she is staying with friends who have lent her a tiny room, but I am to stay with neighbours for a while.

If my mother has a room, why doesn't she let me stay with her?

I ask her. She answers, very embarrassed, evasive, that a child's presence is undesirable. Really, I find all that rather hard to understand.

In fact my mother had run into a childhood friend (an ex-suitor) who had remained single, and he had suggested to my mother that they live together, and I must have been in the way...

A short time afterwards, we get our flat back, I go and live with them. We never speak of my father. I visibly deteriorate, my mother grows alarmed. She blames everything on hardship.

She doesn't understand at all. The doctor advises the open air. I leave for the mountains in Haute Savoie, I spend the best part of a year in a family of farmers. That is where I realised I was Jewish... and what being Jewish meant. We were no longer under the occupation, people knew I was Jewish and they made my life a misery, with their stupid remarks. Completely idiotic, literally astonished that I was physically built as they were. They didn't make any effort to include me in their family life; what's more, they called me 'the stranger'. I felt extremely rebellious. They wanted me to go to catechism classes with their children, to mass, I firmly opposed them.

I wrote to my mother about all this, she thought that it was unimportant, adding that only my health mattered.

It was at this time that I received a letter from a cousin of my father's, who kindly took an interest in me. He told me that he had gone back to observing the Jewish traditions at home, he kept the Sabbath.

I asked him to send me all the books he could lay his hands on that would teach me Jewish history and Hebrew. I taught myself Hebrew, I was very proud. I wrote and told my mother who ignored my letter.

When I went back to Paris I asked to be sent to a Jewish school; my mother gave in, reluctantly, she thought it was a stupid idea, she only spoke French at home: "We must become assimilated and forget all that has happened".

She found some excuse, my health, or the lack of variety in the food, to take me away from the school and send me to a state school: I was a year ahead of my age. A year or two later, my mother remarried legally: my stepfather got it into his head that I too should change my name to his. I howled. I was in such a rage that they didn't pursue the matter any further.

When I am fourteen, my mother, suffering from cancer, explains that she will not live much longer. He wants me to change my name, it has become an obsession. My mother's relatives ask me to go through with the formalities. He wants to keep me with him when I become an orphan.

Two days before my mother's death, I gave in. He adopted me. But I only tagged his name on after mine. Then I lived with him: the blackest period... my mother no longer there to act as a buffer between us.

I studied hard.

I was already a resident medical student when I met my wife. He didn't like her as she wasn't Jewish. And yet she had worn the star, because she had a Jewish grandmother, she had lived in the most Jewish sector of Paris, the rue des Rosiers, and she wanted to convert to Judaism. A strange excuse coming from a man who wanted to be considered totally assimilated. I stood my ground, he never wanted to see us again, I took the necessary steps to dissociate his name from mine. I never had been able to stand him.

You see, I was only nine, and within a week I had to realise that I would never see my father again. He is dead, and, what's more, he died in the "furnaces". You try to imagine those furnaces you can't (like Joan of Arc perhaps?) What had he done to deserve being burnt like that?

You don't ask any questions, you sense that you must not ask "Why", why that other man; has your mother already forgotten her husband. You sense that you are in their way, particularly his. He doesn't like to hear that I am the spitting image of the man who had been his rival, whom he wants to obliterate, even down to his name... and his fatherhood.

I have remained incurably shy, I hate being separated from my children. I called my eldest son after my father. I must admit that I never speak of my father to anyone. He is inside me, that is all, that is enough. I never look at photographs of the past.

But I have remained raw, I have a temper, I fly into terrible rages, if ever I have the impression that someone grudges my individuality in the least degree.

I am very reserved, my wife often complains about it. I do not know how to share anything emotionally, only anger, it is almost hatred.

Finally, beneath my submissive exterior, I suffer, I do not want to think about it, or show it. I am a rebel, and I am afraid, sometimes, of the violence I feel.

I hope that my children will continue to be Jewish, whatever happens. For my part, I have no illusions; what took place can happen again. We are only entitled to a respite, a reprieve between two...

Hear a song in Yiddish... it's impossible, I'd dissolve into tears.

It is very painful, you see?

***

I phoned you yesterday, you are going on holiday this evening, you are very busy. I realise that and yet you insisted on giving this interview, without putting it off...

Yes, I knew that it would be painful, but as it's you who are tackling this subject, I had to help you, absolutely, I haven't the right to get out of it, nor perhaps do I want to... You see, participating in this dissertation is like giving blood to a friend who needs it.

Blood?

Yes... well, a 'source of life'.

PAUL

You know, we're going to talk, but what about? I have the feeling that it's not even worth thinking about, especially that period. I've never talked about it, not even to my wife, and especially, not to my mother, and I try never to think about it. So, I agreed to this interview, because it's you. That's right, I didn't want you to think I wasn't capable of facing up to it, I don't want to run away.

Besides, I know why I don't want to think about my father. You see, I may as well tell you right away, the others no doubt think of their deported parents with love, with respect, whereas I think of my father as a "poor devil".

Deep down, I can't forgive him for being so stupid as to let himself be trapped like an idiot, you see! He ought to have thought more carefully! I think that's what upsets me the most.

To come back to the interview, it'll be very short. It's straightforward. In 1939 we leave for Royan: why? Perhaps because your father took all your family down there: my mother was alone with me, your father took charge of us, that is what I discovered later, when I met you in the first year at Medical School and your name upset my mother.

There we joined my father at Bacarès. He enlisted in the Foreign Legion, as did all Jews at that time. And when I saw him, badly dressed, sad, dirty, coping badly with the situation, I'd have preferred not to have seen him like that. I haven't forgotten that image, and it makes me feel uneasy, as does everything else about my father.

Another image, we have come back to Paris and my father gives me the worst scolding I have ever had. He has made a hiding place inside a double cupboard door: if the police come (they were only looking for men at that time) he will hide in there. I think that is very clever, and I tell all my street mates. I boast of my father's skill and cunning, and I describe the device in detail; one of my friends' parents tells my mother.

Now, when I think of that cupboard, it was ridiculous, it didn't hold together!

I was disturbed, agitated, a bad pupil at kindergarten. At home I only spoke Yiddish, I must have mixed the two languages up at first! Yes, it was only later that I became extremely reasonable, very studious, and a good pupil. I could no longer allow myself to be otherwise.

I don't remember whether I wore the star: in any case, my father leaves, there are many raids, he arrives in the unoccupied zone, he arranges for my mother and me to join him. Finally, he was never with me when I needed comforting, when I was afraid. So, I can picture myself crossing the demarcation line.

My mother makes me cross first; I am the young cousin of a woman who puts me on the carrier of her bicycle. You know, it's so vivid, I have the impression I can still feel the bars of the carrier cutting into my thighs. But suddenly we come across a road block. I have a lump in my throat, the woman says: "we have to go through the woods, we are going to walk, it's a long way, don't dawdle." This is unexpected, and I wonder if I am going to see my mother again. We had seen the block from a distance, but would my mother, who was crossing with another *passeur**, be able to avoid it too?

It seems we have been walking for ages. A German patrol in the forest. But this woman remains unruffled, she thrusts me against a tree and tells me to pee... and tells the Germans that we have left the road because I had to relieve myself.

Passeurs were people who were paid to smuggle Jews into the unoccupied zone.

Fortunately for me, it is dark, I can't urinate, no matter how hard I try. And I have been circumcized, but neither she nor I know that.

We set off again. We arrive two hours later than expected. My mother is waiting for us, she is in a state. When she sees me arrive at last, she weeps buckets!

We live in a small room. I go to school. We are in the unoccupied zone. No star, no memories.

Or rather, yes: at the village school I don't dare ask the teacher if I can be excused and I come home with soiled trousers. My father cannot stand that. He wallops me, he cannot understand what on earth is the matter with me. He is profoundly upset by my attitude.

Finally, it seems that my father was gentle, thoughtful... but the two memories I have of him are: two thrashings. All the same it's rather odd.

One morning, my father receives a summons, it's the end of 1943. He must report to the police station. Later my mother told me she had begged him not to go; he took no notice. He had admitted he was Jewish, if he didn't answer the summons, what would happen to the rest of the family?

And so, you see, it's unbearable, he sacrificed himself for us! I owe him my life twice over.

Supposing he had thought of getting false papers, instead of making it known that he was a Jew, that way he would have saved all of us, yes, he would!

He was deported during the months that followed, he wrote from the train to Auschwitz: "Don't be afraid, I'll survive."

When my mother learnt that he had been taken away, she let herself go to pieces, she wouldn't eat, she was wasting away, she wouldn't speak to me, couldn't hear anything.

I was very frightened. I thought to myself, "I'm going to lose her too!" Some neighbours told me not to go to school, they were rounding up children. My mother was bewildered. For more than a month, I was the one who spoonfed her, it was awful! I had the impression that she would never get back to normal. I was nine, I was looking after her as if she were my child!

A Jewish family who lived not far away came to see us. They had heard about our predicament. They talked with my mother, they told her to change her identity, and, all of a sudden, she became her old self again.

We went to Savoie, to stay with relatives. My mother had regained her composure. Some Catholic friends looked around for a farm to send me to, as if I were their cousin from the North, in need of fresh air. I have another name; I tend the goats. Sometimes my mother sees me. I contrive to take the goats past the house where she is living with her cousins. In accordance with her instructions, I don't look up.

Solitude suited me; I was left in peace, I simply had to make sure that nothing happened to the goats, and goats don't always do as they are told. One day I lost one, I was crying so hard, I didn't dare go back; supposing they didn't want me any more? I knew it was of vital importance!

Fortunately, I found it (I've hated goats ever since!). In this family, I was the only child, they had two sons: one was a collaborator, they never spoke his name; and the other was the leader of the local Resistance forces.

When he occasionally came to the house in the evening, to spend a few hours with his parents, we shut ourselves in, and spoke in low voices, I was part of their family, I was in on the secrets. I was speechless with admiration for this son! When he arrived, the whole house came alive.

Unfortunately, one day he was killed. His parents started drinking, more and more. Our Catholic friend had to find me another family. It wasn't the same. There I tended the cows; luckily, I had a dog, he was my companion.

After Liberation, I tell them I am Jewish, I am going to see my mother again. I stay on the farm until my mother finds us somewhere to live, manages to earn a little money. She comes to fetch me at the beginning of the school year. I am thirteen. I am hopeless at dictation, at sums. I start at the Collège Turgot, I feel humiliated by my backwardness; I very soon make up for it.

My mother waits for my father; I don't: I have become resigned to the fact. I'm the one who has to comfort her.

I have never forgiven my mother for bringing a man into our house, six months after our return, without consulting me: I had to accept him: I rejected him, totally. And my mother with him.

So, I withdrew into myself, I became even more taciturn. I had to succeed in my studies and get out!

My wife is Jewish, I don't think I could have felt happy with someone who wasn't Jewish. My wife's parents were friends of my parents. They spoke to me of my father!

I hope my daughter will marry a Jewish boy. And yet I am an atheist, I no longer believe in anything. I have never been to Israel. Deep down I'm afraid of being disappointed. I have studied the history of the Jewish people. Forever beginning again: persecution, humiliation, flight in order to survive and, above all, to ensure the survival of the children.

I am not "ashamed to be a Jew" but I am not proud of being a Jew either. I don't think any good can come from being Jewish, it can only cause others to misunderstand and to reject my identity, that is, to reject me.

So I have few friends. Perhaps through fear of being disappointed? I have no idea.

In fact, I find it painful to accept my Jewishness, but I accept it. And the humanism, our particular sensitivity, sense of humour, tenderness, the unconditional idealism of the Jews are things which, in spite of everything, help us to live and they are important to me.

MADELEINE AND JOSEPH
1. Madeleine,
Joseph's sister

I was born in 1931 in Paris. I remember my father clearly; after all, I was ten in 1941 when he left for the camp at Pithiviers.

I'm going to admit something appalling to you. I can't forgive him, I can't forgive my father for letting himself be deported without trying to escape his fate. I know that what I'm telling you is disgraceful, but, as I am talking about it today, I must tell you what I haven't been able to get off my chest for thirty five years, you understand?

My parents hadn't yet obtained naturalization. In 1941 my father received a summons from the police. It was stipulated that if he didn't report to the police station, sanctions would be taken against the rest of his family.

All right, I'll allow that he was right to have gone, but afterwards... He could have escaped from Pithiviers. He didn't!

He worked privately for some people a few miles from the camp. He had become friendly with them and when my mother and I went to visit him, he insisted on coming to the railway station with us: he had given his word to those people that he would go back. They were responsible for him. One day my mother brought a train ticket for him, she begged him to run away, to come back with us: he refused. He didn't want to betray these people's confidence. They would have to pay for the consequences. You see what kind of man he was? He was an idealist, an idealistic tailor.

He was intelligent, interested in everything, he read widely.
He was an active member of *Bund*, a Jewish, socialist
organization. He believed in many things. That's what killed
him, he wouldn't make concessions, not even at Auschwitz.

We learned from other deportees that he had been
designated 'kapo' by the S.S. You know, 'kapo' meant being
the Jewish S.S. over the other Jews. He refused. He threw
himself against the electrified barbed-wire fence that same
evening. He committed suicide.

At least he chose his own death. He had been deported in
1942, among the first, he didn't suffer the ordeal of the
concentration camps, you see? That's my only consolation.

You have to admit he preserved a sense of moral values,
right up to his death, didn't he? But all the same, his life was
more important! But I'd have preferred a live father, even if
his survival had cost him his principles, to the image of a dead
martyr-father.

It's awful, isn't it? But that's what I think, and if he were
here, that's what I'd tell him to his face.

Preserve a sense of moral values in that hell! He didn't
know how to adapt himself to what is inhuman. And I, his
daughter, I hold that against him. It's appalling!

It took your dissertation for me to be entitled for once in
my life to get it off my chest. At least that, yes, at least that.

However, he had told my mother who to go to, should we
be in trouble. He was convinced that his organization would
help us, and in that, he was right. They did help us, they
procured false identity cards for us, gave us addresses, money
and arranged for us to cross to Switzerland. So, you see, my
brother and I owe him our lives. We were penniless, without
contacts. It was for his sake that people bent over backwards,
he was certainly greatly loved and respected.

But I'm telling you all this haphazardly. I can't bring
myself to tell you about my own experience.

On the morning of the great raid of the *Vél'd'Hiv*, that is in
July 1942, (my father's organization had warned us of the
imminence of that raid), someone banged on the door,
repeated loud knocks. I was in the toilet. I pulled the chain.

My mother, with remarkable presence of mind, dashed to turn off the water supply at the main, in the kitchen. Fortunately. We had been told not to open up, not to move, but to stay locked in.

Our neighbour from across the hall then came out and told them that the husband had been taken away to a camp, and that the wife and two children had left to stay with relatives in the country, a good while ago.

They didn't insist, but she heard the chief say that they would have to come back. She immediately procured food for us, for the coming days. We weren't to make a sound. They came back three or four times that same day. I was scared to death... and I kept wanting to go to the toilet.

That evening, the neighbour had an idea: a tenant on the fifth floor had gone away, I don't know where, and had left her the keys to the flat. We were going to move in. My mother packed the barest minimum, mainly clothes, as she thought, and rightly so, that we wouldn't be returning to our flat. We had to leave that house no later than the following day, and let my aunt know of our arrival. My aunt had nothing to fear; she was Jewish but French. From our house to hers, twenty minutes on foot. It was our neighbour who went to inform her.

The following morning, my mother dressed me in a heavy coat, two jackets, two dresses and a skirt, explaining that I had to keep the coat buttoned up, with a shawl over my shoulders, to conceal the star. I was to walk in front of her, but if anything happened to her, if she was arrested on the way, I was to carry on walking whatever happened, without looking round; I had to promise her that!

Even if she was arrested, she said, with my brother in her arms, they would let her go. I had to do as I was told, without any argument. I had no reason to be afraid. Nobody would guess that a little girl with such fair hair and such light eyes was a little Jewish girl, as long as the star was not visible, she added.

So, I walked two hundreds yards ahead of my mother. I was shaking from head to foot, I was scared to death, I felt as though my legs would give way under me. I arrived at my aunt's, my mother joined me not even five minutes later; I had a fit of hysterics on arrival, it took a long time to calm me down.

It was mid-July, in the strong heat, that little girl, dressed as if it were the depths of winter... that was enough to make people notice me, in spite of my fair hair and light eyes.

What a morning! It must have been around ten o'clock when I went to the window to watch. There was an outcry coming from the street. I saw a man, the same age as my father, that the police were trying to take away, he was howling, struggling, then he allowed himself to be dragged along the ground. That has remained the most horrible scene I've ever witnessed. I can't forget it. I began to shriek in the flat as if I were mad, it was already more than I could bear.

That same evening, we were to leave for the unoccupied zone, by train. We were to travel with a man (paid by the organization): we were his children, my mother was his sister-in-law. They drummed that into me. My brother was too young, he represented no threat.

My mother didn't receive the papers in time. I remember, the man was furious. We didn't leave until the next day. We were to travel first class. He asked my mother to dress as elegantly as possible. She wasn't without charm, she wore a very fine hat belonging to my aunt. Missing the train the day before had been a blessing in disguise, they had gone through it with a tooth-comb. And my mother had a strong accent that wouldn't have fooled anybody.

There were inspections on our train. Not in our compartment. We arrived in Lyon.

While we were waiting to leave for Switzerland, the organization advised mummy to send us to a castle where there were only Jewish children. My brother had measles. I wasn't allowed to go near him; I went to see him in secret.

Then we left for Switzerland. In our group there was a couple with a baby, another couple with a five or six year old child, my mother and ourselves. Of the journey itself, I remember nothing. My mother had to carry my brother in her arms during the entire journey: he was heavy, so the *passeur* took over when she was worn out, he sat him on his shoulders. My brother was very pleased. Then the *passeur* dropped us, we had to carry on without him, we were at the frontier, all we had to do was walk straight ahead.

It was night time, we must have walked round in circles, we found ourselves confronted by two Italian *carabinieri*; we were done for! There was my mother and ourselves, the young couple with the baby. The other couple had stopped for a few minutes because the little boy couldn't go on any more; they saw that we'd been caught. They stayed hidden amongst the trees.

Then my mother started to beg the *carabinieri*, she indicated the baby and us two, I don't know if they were fathers themselves, they weren't Germans, they took pity on us. They showed us which way to go. Ten minutes later we were in Switzerland, near Annemasse.

Two or three days later we were in a refugee camp, and after a week or so, we were told that families had been found for the children. We had to be separated from my mother. We took the train with other children, our names on cards hanging round our necks. When we got off the train, our host families were waiting for us. That was when I realised that my brother and I were going to be split up. But his family and mine knew each other.

The family wasn't very nice to me: most of the time I didn't eat with them. I went to school, where only Swiss-German was spoken; I was lost, my mother wasn't allowed to visit us at first. I made the beds, did the washing up, peeled the vegetables for the whole household, and worst of all, I had to polish the father's and the son's hunting boots, they were very muddy.

I wasn't allowed to have my chocolate ration. Only the eldest daughter, who was studying in Zurich, spoiled me; when she came home for the holidays, she gave me her own ration. I still write to her, she has met my husband, my sons. She didn't get on with her parents, she didn't approve of the way her mother treated me. I received more than my fair share of slaps.

And so, the first time I saw my mother, I asked her to find me another family. Six months later, I was with a different family, where I wasn't asked to do any housework, no-one took any notice of me, they gave me my chocolate, they treated me with total indifference. I preferred that, any day!

Then, when Liberation came, my mother went back to Paris, alone, my brother and I stayed on in Switzerland for a few months, we were to go back with the children's convoys.

One Sunday, in Zurich, some friends of my parents came to see me. They had a daughter my age. Everyone was talking, Marguerite and I in French, her parents in Yiddish. At one point they started speaking Polish, I was walking next to them, I looked at them, I said: "My father's dead, isn't he? That's why you're speaking in Polish..." Their protests were useless, suddenly I was certain of what was going on.

When I went back, my mother took me with her to the Hotel Lutetia; she still believed my father would come back. I was with her when a friend of my parents recognized her and told her how my father had killed himself.

My uncle came to live with us. He was my mother's sister's husband. His wife and daughters had been deported. He was alone. The Jewish tradition that a widow should remarry, quickly, and if possible, a member of the family, was being upheld.

At home, he and I were constantly at odds, for no reason. My mother tried to smooth the situation. It was unbearable. I had the feeling, when he looked at me, that he hated me. I looked very much like his daughter, my cousin. He must have thought: "Why is she alive, and not my daughter?" Besides, I thought, "Why is he alive, and not my father?" My father, whose place he was taking.

He didn't squabble with my brother. He called me a slacker, I wasn't very bright at school, but I'd have liked to continue my studies. I was only good at German!

My mother and my uncle took over the management of a baker's. They needed a hand, so they asked me to leave school. We didn't stop arguing, I spent the whole day with them. My uncle must have regretted having me for an assistant.

I was twenty when I got married.

I have never been a "well adjusted" person, as they say. I hide it as best I can, acquaintances find me gay, gregarious, full of life. In fact, I keep everything inside me, I am unhappy, I often cry when I am alone.

I've had suicidal impulses. But this is the first time I've realised it... when there was a question of separation, from my husband, or my eldest son.

And yet, I knew that they would come back and that there was no longer anything to be afraid of.

You see, I have never really got over the War. I'm afraid of lots of things, I feel anguished sometimes, even a sort of panic, that I have difficulty explaining; I feel very much alone, even isolated. Quite abandoned in fact.

My brother, however, was much luckier. I think he was too young to understand, so he came through it much better. And yet, he won't allow us to talk about daddy in his hearing, he can't seem to bear it either! It's strange!

I'm glad you're doing this dissertation. You know, it's like the death of deported relatives... perhaps it isn't "in vain"... I'm going to be a grandmother shortly, I only hope that this child won't experience all that we suffered. That's my only wish for its start in life.

MADELEINE AND JOSEPH
II. Joseph,
Madeleine's brother

I don't remember my father. I only know him from photographs; I was four when he went away.

In any case, I've often thought that in losing my father, I had lost my home and mother at one go. This may sound surprising, but I consider my mother to be my mother only in name, but that's all. I have nothing in common with her. My real mother is my Swiss mother, as I call her.

You know, we had barely settled in at the camp in Switzerland before they separated the children from their parents. The fashion had definitely caught on.

So, they put us on a train, we are on our way to our new families: my second mother and I fell in love at first sight: I thought she was very pretty! She was a "spinster", aged about forty, with an open face glowing with goodness (she's seventy seven now, I often see her, but she is ill, I'm worried about her). She is the only person who has ever given me any warmth and affection.

She had dreamed of having a son, and I, of having a mother like her. It was a piece of luck for both of us. She only spoke a few words of French; and I had never heard Swiss-German before, but we understood each other perfectly well.

I only lived with her for three years. When I had to leave, that's when I experienced separation. I cried, so did she, I swore I'd do everything I could to come back very soon. . . and I believed I would.

In the evenings, she would tell me stories; during the day,

she took an interest in me, in my progress, she was proud of me.

I spoke Swiss like a native, so well that I completely forgot French.

So, my return was quite something! Total anti-climax! A mother who couldn't grasp the situation; I was made to feel like an intruder. After two days I had understood that she wasn't interested in me. My sister? We had nothing in common. And my uncle-step-father, he was the last straw! Fortunately there were two of us who spoke Swiss-German: and my sister, who hadn't forgotten her French, translated for me.

Perpetual quarrelling between my sister and my uncle, my mother acting as buffer; and nobody took any notice of me... Whole days went past without a single word being spoken in my direction, I didn't have any little friends. My mother left to go to the baker's shop and I, to go to school; she didn't worry about whether I got home all right nor at what time. Not to mention the fact that no-one asked me how I was getting on at school. It was too much!

I was sent to a primary school. At first, as I didn't understand French, I fell asleep on my desk, the teacher left me alone.

She asked my mother to come to the school two or three times. My mother forgot she had an appointment, or she couldn't make it. This teacher must have talked about me to her colleagues; the fact remains that a teacher from one of the higher classes, who knew German, asked me to come and work with him every day; he was going to teach me French. Do you know what his name was? Monsieur Lallemand*...

And for a year, refusing to accept any money, he sat with me at lunch time and during the evening study period. He saved me, he taught me to read and to write, and he stood by me, a real friend. So much so, that one day, I dragged him to the baker's shop, I wanted my mother to thank him, as the school year was drawing to a close. I was so embarassed by the

*L'allemand in French means 'the German'.

welcome he received that. . . it was the last time I took a friend home.

A charming detail: because I only spoke German, the kids in my area had nicknamed me the "little Boche". I talked to this teacher about it, he put a stop to it.

Then he left for the provinces, I found myself even more alone. I wrote to my Swiss mother, I hoped to spend my holidays with her. It was out of the question; journeys cost money; we didn't have any. I couldn't go and see her until three or four years later. It was extraordinary, I had come home.

My mother had difficulty accepting this relationship. She was very jealous. Stupidly jealous, that's all.

I felt stifled at home; so I spent all my time outdoors, I came home at all hours, as long as it was before nine in the evening, no-one said anything. I spent entire Thursdays outside, no-one could be bothered to ask where I had been.

I had found a photo of my father, and I remember how, in the evenings, I used to hide it under the blanket, and I often cried over it, life wasn't exactly gay.

I was never taken out, to the cinema, to the park, to the zoo, well, the things that other children do!

My uncle liked going to the greyhound races, once a week. It was the big family outing.

One day I had had enough, enough. I left the house, I walked, and walked; at eleven o'clock at night I arrived exhausted at my aunt's. I couldn't swallow any food, I needed to sleep. . . nothing else. My aunt let my mother know I was there. Apparently she had been very worried, for quite a while. I must have been thirteen or fourteen. I hadn't left after a row, or because of any particular grievance, no, I simply couldn't stand living with them any longer. I didn't want to go back there. I stayed with my aunt for nearly a week, then I went home, nobody ever referred to this incident.

Then my sister met my future brother-in-law, he brought me back to life. It was better than having an elder brother; he was young, but I wished he could have been my father. He took an interest in me, I felt that I mattered to him. I had someone to talk to, to discuss things with. It was he who found me my first job, who always advised me; it's true, he brought me back to life.

As my uncle had died, I stayed with my mother, at home. I ate there and slept there, that's all. She and I were separated by a wall.

I had nightmares; what's more, I still wake up during the night, in tears, although less and less frequently; I am near Auschwitz, I can hear a sort of wailing, I am with other people, I say: "Stop, someone's shouting in there." They stare at me as if I am mad: "Come, come, there's no longer anything here, it's deserted," they reply. But I can't leave with them... I ask them to leave me there, alone, and as soon as I'm on my own, dreadful cries, a sort of wailing, start up again and I can make out human shapes in a haze of smoke... so the crematorium is still functioning, the truth has been hidden from me?... and I wake up crying, in a state of panic.

My wife was alarmed when I told her, one day, if I have to die, I'd rather my children died at the same time. I had to explain that to lose one's father is not very good for a child. You must admit that to be fatherless when you know that your father died "naturally" is bad enough! But then, you change families, country, language, background at the age of five. Three years later the same thing happens all over again, and once more you don't speak the same language as everybody else; you get your uncle as a step-father; you haven't a clue who you are, where you live, why everything is "back-to-front". It's hard!

You know, I'm not glad to be Jewish, not at all. As an anti-religious atheist, Judaism exasperates me. As for the sentimental side, it's even worse: the idea that my father died because he was a Jew has stayed with me: so how do you expect me to feel happy being a Jew?

Once, I had a very strange reaction: I've never been to Israel, but when the six-day war broke out, I wanted to enlist as a volunteer. You'll never guess why: in Israel they have planted a tree for each deportee; I had to go and defend my father's tree, it was as though his life was going to be taken from him a second time, or his grave violated; I don't know how to explain what I felt, but I wanted to scream, to scream endlessly.

Apart from that tree, my father left me a sense of moral values. And, for my part, I'm proud that he refused to be 'kapo', they didn't succeed in breaking him.

I've wanted to commit suicide, particularly when I was a teenager... but I never took the plunge; I would have been ashamed with respect to my father, he'd have sacrificed his life in vain!

I owe him my life. If he hadn't been who he was, his friends wouldn't have gone out of their way to save us, as they did. It was for my father's sake that they did it, not for ours!

Apparently my father was cheerful. I regret not knowing how to laugh or play with my children; I'm not used to it, no doubt; I think you have to learn how to enjoy yourself, like learning French... My mother maintains that I wasn't affected by the War, that I didn't miss my father... because I don't remember him.

Are there any Jewish children who weren't "affected"?

SAMUEL

I don't know why I agreed to this interview. Perhaps because I hadn't seen you for years. It was an excuse to see each other again, to spend an evening together. You haven't even seen my youngest son. But, all the same, I'd have preferred to meet you to talk about something else.

In fact, it's not the subject that worries me, it's the psychiatric aspect! Yes, I detest anything to do with psychiatry, with psycho-analysis.

Perhaps you don't know. I may as well tell you right away, my eldest son, the son from my first marriage, has been in a home for two years, he's being treated for "schizophrenia". It's awful!

I haven't really anything interesting to tell you... It's so commonplace! I was born in 1933; I have an elder sister; we lived in the North.

My parents had a clothes shop, my father was a furrier. We were quite well off, I think.

My father was called up. He asked my mother to leave with us for Paris, where he joined us much later.

I don't think anybody wore the star yet when we left for the unoccupied zone. I don't remember.

I only recall crossing the demarcation line. My father had crossed first; I was with my mother and sister. We had to walk, walk for a long time, and not make a sound. I don't think I was afraid, I was just very tired.

First of all we went to Nice. No memories of Nice, nothing.

Then in 1943 we ended up in Lyon. Why? I don't know.

I didn't wear the star, because in Lyon I changed my name: not my surname, but my first name: it was in fact my middle name. I've kept it ever since. My surname sounds very French. My parents spoke without a trace of an accent. Only my first name, a Biblical name, was a danger.

Before changing my name, I was a bright pupil and I was ahead of my age. Strange thing, when I changed my name, I found myself at the bottom of the class.

In Lyon we lived in a tiny two-roomed flat, a sort of converted loft.

My father had joined the Resistance. In what capacity, I don't know.

I only know that it was cold and that my father was making lumber-jackets for the *maquisards**...

One evening, around five o'clock, he went to deliver them to the appointed address. He was caught by the Gestapo. The whole Resistance network was dismantled at the same time. It was the 31st of January 1944.

I was ashamed to say that my father had been deported. I could picture those cattle trains, and then those striped pyjamas and the shorn heads of the deportees, their grotesqueness. I was ashamed. So I always told the other children that my father had been arrested as a Resistant, and shot by the Germans. I don't understand why I was ashamed of his death!

He was deported to Auschwitz on the 7th of March 1944. I heard afterwards that with the last convoys, the people who had survived the journey were gassed on arrival. You know the system: they were given a towel, supposedly for a shower. The business was over.

It never occurred to me that he wouldn't come back! You know, my father was resourceful, and then, physically – I take after him – he was over six foot, he was very sporty. What's more, March 1944, the War was nearly over.

During the last holidays before the War, my father and I

* Underground forces.

went fishing, just the two of us.

I can't go on with this interview. It's too painful. (*And Samuel breaks down, he sobs desperately, his head on the table, hidden in his hands. His sobs continue for more than half an hour, he doesn't even try to restrain himself. Amidst his sobs, a groan, very childlike: "Daddy, Daddy," recurs two or three times. All of a sudden, Samuel stops crying; he says in one breath:*) You can't understand, nobody knows about it. The only time I ever had an argument with my father, when he left, angry, without our having made up, was the evening of his arrest. Do you understand how much I blame myself? And I was the one in the wrong. I didn't want to give up the comic I was reading, even though I had another one.

He was mad about strip cartoons. What got into me? He left, angry at me. An argument, that's how I said goodbye to my father. My God, he didn't deserve that either, he was gentle, and so patient with me... that I no doubt took advantage of him... And so, that evening, we waited, and waited... My sister went to find out what had happened.

I was told by a neighbour. I didn't realise anything! That evening we went to sleep at the house of some friends, we left all our belongings in the converted attic, and the following morning my mother, my sister and I left for a village, perhaps in Savoie.

When France was liberated, we were involved in a rather strange incident. I was very frightened then. Some *maquisards* turned up at our house. They thought my mother was a German spy, and wanted to take her away! One day they had come across her speaking Yiddish with my aunt. No way of convincing them. I was alone with my mother. I don't know what would have happened if my sister hadn't arrived at that moment. My sister was sixteen, and already very beautiful. The leader listened to her. They went out together afterwards, and he then confessed that he had let my mother go because of my sister's pretty face, but at that point, he didn't believe we were speaking the truth. I, however, had clearly sensed the danger of the situation. Much more so than the fact that I was Jewish, or that my father had been arrested!

My mother had nothing left: no money, no shop, no home; she had no news of my father; she didn't know what to do with me. She heard of a children's home, set up to help mothers on their own. I stayed there for more than six months.

Later, my mother remarried. My step-father, who had lost his four sisters at Auschwitz, had a niece. She became my first wife. I got married very young, I was beginning my studies, she was pregnant. But I didn't get married because it was an obligation, not at all. We were deeply in love. She hadn't turned seventeen, I wasn't yet nineteen; we were both very disturbed.

My son was ten when we divorced. She remarried, this time a non-Jewish factory worker.

My son didn't get on with his step-father. As soon as I married again, he came to live with us. I got married to a Jewish girl, of North African origin, who knew nothing of the War. I have three other children.

My eldest son blames us, we didn't give him what he needed. It cost my father his life, my son is also paying, in a different, but just as harsh, way. And I haven't been spared. I don't like being apart from my children, even for the holidays.

For me, the 31st of January is seldom just another day.

You know, since my father left, I've never been able to cry. I felt walled in. I had forgotten that I was even able to cry!

Five or six years ago, when I had already married a second time, there was a programme on the television one day: it was about two or three Jewish women who had lost their families through deportation, and the object of the programme was to find out how they adapted to their new life as housewife and mother.

My first wife agreed to take part in the programme. She said that for her, it was the past, that she was happily married with two delightful little daughters, whom she talked about a lot. That evening, my eldest son was watching the television with us. She didn't mention him...

It was the following morning that he had his first fit. I have always wondered whether there was a relation between cause and effect; but in any case, he was already unsettled. You know, I didn't really want to talk about it!

PAULETTE AND CHARLES
A COUPLE
I. Paulette

You know, I agreed to do this interview, but I'm scared... I'm even very scared. In fact, if it hadn't been for you, I would never have agreed. And yet, deep down, I hope I'll feel better afterwards; what's more I don't know why...

I can't contribute anything very interesting, my life is so ordinary... It's the same as for everybody else: I was in hiding, my father was deported, and he didn't come back, my mother found a replacement, quickly, without any fuss. But I didn't want a replacement. That's all, I've told you everything.

But what else...

My brother and I were born in Alsace, he in 1935, and I in 1937. Do you know the only memory I have of my father? I wouldn't eat, my mother was trying to make me, I rushed towards my father who was entering the room, he was tall... I ran between his legs, he protected me with his arms... and I can still see my father's strong legs.

Only my elder brother mattered to my mother, she still idolizes him.

I realise that I'm spouting all this haphazardly, in no logical order, it's dreadful. I hope you'll be able to make sense of it. Because I can't see very clearly in all this mess.

Where were we in 1941? I haven't a clue. I can only remember being at T... We lived with my mother in a small flat; my brother and I went to school on our own, it was a long way; I went to the kindergarten, with him I think, or else it was

a day-nursery... Anyway I remember a neighbour had said to
my mother: "You don't allow two children aged four and six
to go to school on their own, not when there are roads to
cross."

I think that my mother had managed to find work
somewhere; my father wasn't with us.

Then she sent us to a farm. We had false identity cards...
but I don't remember whether we used them or not... it's
hazy, it's so hazy...

The farmers were kindly towards us, or at least, they weren't
hostile. I must have stayed with them for about a year and a
half, perhaps two years, don't remember anything... All the
same, that's odd, because when I left, I was nearly eight...

My mother came to see us once or twice. During all that
period I asked where Daddy was, why he didn't come and see
us, my mother burst into tears without answering, that I do
remember.

That has always been her way of replying... so I didn't ask
any more questions.

After Liberation, I was still on the farm, I waited
impatiently for my parents to come back. I had a dream there
that I've never forgotten: I had a loose tooth, and then another
one, I was crying, and upset, I was frightened that all my teeth
would fall out. Then my father arrived, picked me up,
comforted me, he brought me sweets and cakes...

Now, the next day, one of my teeth fell out... and in the
evening it was my mother who came, with no cakes or sweets.
What's more, she wasn't alone; she was with my father's
brother. (It seems to me I had never seen him before the war;
and yet he only lived about seventy miles away from us).

Mummy came to get us from the farm, only to send my
brother, cousin and myself to a Jewish children's home in
Versailles immediately afterwards. We stayed there for over a
year. I was happy there, even very happy. I felt at ease, I was
cheerful, I had friends. All the people who looked after us
coddled us, they gave us a semblance of family life.

At Versailles, I realised I was Jewish (I never wore the star)
but there, I also admitted that I would never see my father

again. All the children there were in the same situation, they were still waiting for their parents to come back. The principal of the home sometimes tried to raise the matter: a complete waste of time, I think, as none of the children wanted to talk about all that. I learnt Jewish history, and the little Hebrew that I know; we celebrated all the holidays, we sang, we danced. I became very religious and practising...

That is when my mother and my uncle came to fetch us, we were going back to Alsace. Mummy had retrieved our old house. She never told us that our uncle was coming to live with us; we didn't talk about those things, we just had to put up with them.

We were enrolled at the school... you know what, it was a convent. We were coming from a Jewish home where the religion, the traditions were observed in earnest.

The nuns allowed us to be excused from religious instruction; we arrived later in the morning: so the other children begrudged us this favour (apparently no-one had explained it to them), and they called my cousin a "dirty Jew". What a homecoming! My mother immediately sent us to a different school. After that there was no more friction at school. Within the family however...

First of all we had left a loving environment. Here, no-one showed me any sign of affection. The religious side: also abandoned.

When my mother spoke of my father – for now she quoted him all the time – she made him sound the most intelligent man on earth, the best. She turned him into a "sacred cow". He had become "darling Daddy".

According to her mood, she would even announce, "Darling Daddy would like you to do this or that..."

I don't know if I told you how I learned of my father's death. (I think it was just as we were leaving T... for Versailles. My mother had just been officially notified of my father's death at Auschwitz.)

In a real fit of hysterics, she insisted on sharing her suffering with us: she had been told that they had found my father's name scrawled with his own blood on a wall. For years, in fact,

even until well after the birth of my eldest son, I think, I kept
having the same nightmare: I saw my father clinging to a rock
with his bleeding hands, and a German beating him to make
him lose his grip. I would wake up then, in such a state...

It was my uncle who told me how my father had been
caught. It was supper time; my father and my mother were
about to sit down. The police went up to a neighbouring flat,
to arrest people who had been denounced, but who had fled in
time. So they raided the whole building, with an identity
inspection. When the police knocked at the door, my mother
took her papers from her bag and threw them into the soup-
tureen full of steaming soup.

They were taken to the *Kommandantur*. My mother said she
didn't know what she had done with her papers. She said she
was a friend of my father's, not his wife. My father confirmed
her statements; he admitted to being Jewish (besides, he was
circumcized).

My parents understood German very well, they had heard
the chief say: "In her case, I don't know, she doesn't look
Jewish." It's unbelievable. But my mother is tall and fair with
green eyes. They let her go, I don't know how.

But since that day, she has always vomited after every meal:
in fact, on that day she denied the bond that united her to my
father. It's not easy to stomach... I got married, I left Alsace, I
don't look forward to going back on visits.

One day after a particularly violent household row, my
uncle exclaimed: "When I think of how your mother
embellishes the past, you know your parents didn't get on.
There were rows all the time, just as violent as this one..."
They destroyed even that image for me... But I wonder if I
hadn't already realised that by myself, her "Darling Daddy"
had always exasperated me, that way of "mummifying" him,
it was taking from him the little life he had left in my opinion.

This year, when my son had his *Bar Mitzvah*... I thought of
my father, a lot, I was very sad... I didn't have a father, my son
didn't have either of his grandfathers.

PAULETTE AND CHARLES
A COUPLE
II. Charles

You spent such a long time talking to my wife... and yet she was apprehensive about this interview. I'm not. Besides, with me, it'll be over quickly. I no longer remember anything, to such an extent that I don't know if my memories are mine, or if they are something I've been told about.

You know, a few hours after the birth of our eldest son, my wife and I talked about our respective fathers, perhaps because I wanted him to be named after my father; my wife insisted on calling him after her father: two grandfathers deported, that's a lot for an only grandson.

We had been married for five years, we had known each other for seven. On that day we came up with the hypothesis that the two grandfathers might have known each other at Auschwitz, who knows?

Anyway, one thing is certain, they both died there.

That was the only time my wife and I ever spoke about... about that. We couldn't help ourselves, and we very quickly started talking about something else.

My father left us in 1942. He was interned at Drancy, then he managed to escape, with some help.

As he had been naturalized, before Drancy, he thought he was safe. Afterwards, he wondered how to protect his factory, he didn't want it to be occupied.

He saved his factory, but as for himself, he was deported, in spite of his connections, his money, and his French nationality. He always thought he was more intelligent than everyone else, he would never listen to anyone else's advice.

He was a strange character. In fact, when I was a child, I was afraid of him, but I greatly admired him. He arrived fom Poland, penniless; he studied engineering while earning his own living, with great difficulty. At that time he made a discovery, but he wanted to market this invention himself, and have it patented.

Meanwhile, in Paris, he met my mother, who was as lost as he was, apparently, very much alone, (her entire family was still in Warsaw). They got married, they were starving, all their money went on this famous invention.

Thereupon, disaster: my mother became pregnant; so she went back to her mother's in Poland to have the baby. That's where I was born, and I stayed there till the age of four.

By then, my father had managed to get a patent for his invention. Some people had confidence in him, the factory came into being; money and repute along with it. As for him, he began to think he was a little genius. When it was a question of saving his life, his genius wasn't up to the situation.

In 1936 I came back from Poland with my grandmother; I didn't know my parents; and I met my sister, who was born in 1934, for the first time. My father spoke to me very sharply, I no longer understood French, I annoyed them, I wanted to return to Poland with my grandmother, I had been happy there. . . However he was caught up in a social whirl; he wasn't interested in me at all. My sister was very pretty, that, on the other hand, flattered him.

One day, I exasperated him, I don't know what I had done. He hit me very hard, and he stopped in surprise because I shouted: "But I'm Monique's brother, stop!" I can still see that scene.

And then, using something else I did wrong as an excuse, he got rid of me as best he could: he sent me to boarding school, I was seven. I often cried. My mother didn't interfere. My mother kept my sister with her throughout the War, whereas I was sent to a Catholic school, as a boarder: I wasn't unhappy there, but I wasn't happy.

I joined in the Catholic rites, but the Father Superior had

asked me to do so to avoid the suspicions of the other boarders. I had a false identity card (I've always kept that card, by the way), but one day there was a handwriting competition; I had always been top in handwriting, since I was eight or nine, (it's odd, I, who only spoke Polish till I was four); anyway, at this wretched competition, I gave myself away. I was representing the Catholic school, and I wrote my real name on the page. I was the best in the county, I had my name in the local paper!

After that I couldn't stay at the Catholic school. I went back to my mother, who, not knowing what else to do with me, kept me at home with my sister.

You know, everybody went on at me for my blunder, but it's true, I didn't do it on purpose. I was even very frightened when I realised what had happened. I wasn't exactly stupid. Would you believe that ever since that incident, when I had to write my name on an exam paper – but I'm talking about my university studies – I always experienced a moment of panic. And yet there was no danger of my putting down the name on the false identity card, really. Besides, I've completely forgotten it.

Well, it was the only competition I ever won, and I got my name into the papers! I absolutely insisted on sending the article to my father, so that he could be proud of me at least once in his life. He had already been deported; I thought of him as being in prison, and I didn't understand why the letter wouldn't reach him.

Since that memorable competition (I don't know, by the way, why I am going on about it, but I'm sure that it was very important. . .) I have always distinguished myself amongst the last.

You see how, from my father I received no love or affection; he simply rejected me, throughout my childhood. In spite of that, I waited for him to come back, if you only knew how I waited!

Perhaps I was waiting for him to give me what I asked for at last, for him to be a good father to me, for him to come back and tell me everything was going to be all right between us.

Because I hated him sometimes, but I loved him, my father, I loved him... and he, he had always seen to it that I had never been able to tell him all that...

You know my sister is being treated for schizophrenia... she is unrecognizable, mentally and even physically; she missed her father a lot; what's more, he loved her...

I have been very unstable during my life. Until the birth of my children perhaps.

Happiness, I don't know what it is, but I have never known, so... I am withdrawn, subject to fits of rage; though people find me reserved, shy and very gentle for a man.

I still have this nightmare, though much less often however; my father comes back, he gets off one of those sealed trains, with that striped outfit, his head shorn, (he who was so elegant!). He walks past me, I don't recognize him, he's looking for me, he can't see me, I've changed, I've grown, what shall I do? I shout: "Daddy, Daddy!" but hundreds of children are shouting the same thing. Then I have an idea, I shout: "Charles is calling his father, M.G.!" An awful silence follows, in that station: the S.S. rush up to my father, I have spoken his name, I shouldn't have! When I patent one of my inventions... I always think of my father. He passed on some of his talent to me. Part of him is alive in me...

But you know, I'm only the pale reflection of my father. He, in everybody's opinion, was a rather extraordinary man!

I've told you about my father, you see, it's the first time I've ever told anyone about him. But that's not what your *mémoire** is about, is it? What did you want me to talk about? I've forgotten! A *mémoire*, what a funny name!

**mémoire* = both dissertation and memory in French.

MYRIAM

I was born in Paris.

My earliest memory is that of a violent quarrel between my
father and my mother, in Toulouse, where we had taken
refuge. My mother was reproaching my father for going to
Synagogue twice a day. "It wasn't the time to go to
Synagogue", she said, whereas he thought that it was only in
times like these that the Jew prays, so...

My mother was afraid, the round-ups were becoming more
and more frequent. She implored my father to understand
that we shouldn't sleep at the flat that was our stated address.
My father wouldn't listen. In spite of that, my mother had
managed to rent, right over the other side of the town, a tiny
room, and she succeeded in persuading my father to go there
with us. But as soon as he went into that room, he saw a
crucifix above the bed, so, without a word, he left.

Every evening it was the same story. My father refused to
go, my mother took my little sister and me there. We had to
walk for a long time, and quickly: my mother carried my little
sister in her arms, it was very tiring. I was frightened the
whole way. (At that time, my elder sister was in a
convalescent home).

One day, my father begged me to stay at home with him.
"I'll give you a packet of sweets," he said. And so, I agreed;
but when evening came and my mother was getting ready to
leave with my sister, I began to cry, and stamp my foot, I
didn't want the sweets any more, I wanted to leave. My father

said, very calmly, "You promised, now you must stay." For him, hiding like that, even if we hadn't changed our identity, was still a refusal to accept ourselves as Jews. In any case, the question of false identity papers had never arisen, not even my mother brought it up. We were Jewish, that was our fate, and we had to accept it!

One evening, my mother had had enough of these quarrels, of taking us such a long way, she stayed with us and slept in the flat. Around six o'clock in the morning, the Germans arrived. My father had left to go to Synagogue, they arrested him on the way, we ended up in the camp at Toulouse with him. A dreadful scene, a German is striking my mother, who won't budge, before they take us away. I have never been able to talk about that scene with my mother. I still wonder why he persisted in attacking her, as if that wasn't enough... At the camp in Toulouse, hunger and above all, boredom. August 1944: the train towards deportation. When we were perhaps half-way, they separated us: men on one side, women and children on the other. My father said goodbye to us, that scene... I can't bear it.

We, that is, my mother, my young sister and myself, arrive at Buchenwald. No recollection: yes, my mother doesn't want to cut my hair which is very long, and she spends hours looking for lice. But the camp is disorganized, the S.S. can't cope. So, they put us in another sealed carriage, we arrive at Bergen-Belsen. That journey, a nightmare. My mother had managed to save some breadcrumbs for the journey, my sister and I fought bitterly over them.

Bergen-Belsen... I remember one incident, my young sister was very sweet, so my mother sent her to the kitchens to beg a little more soup. Sometimes she was successful and brought back several tinsful, which we shared round.

But my sister falls ill; so my mother asks me to go to the kitchens instead: I refuse; my mother implores me, in vain; it was impossible for me... you see, I understood, I was already six... I assure you, I was fully aware of the situation, I already had been in Toulouse.

Our good fortune was that my mother, was the stabilising

factor, even at Bergen-Belsen. She said that it would all come
to an end, that we would soon go back to Paris, that all we
had to do was wait. I believe that I thought, at that time, that
my mother hadn't understood, or rather, hadn't realised
what was going on!

When we returned from deportation, my mother went to
fetch my older sister from the convalescent home, and then
we stayed in Toulouse for a while, in our old flat. I don't
know why.

Then, very quickly, I had to be sent to a sanatorium; I spent
a year and a half there, and afterwards I went back to Paris.
As soon as I knew how to read, all I asked for were books to
do with the deportation; that was the only thing I was
interested in; by the age of eight, I think I had read everything
there was on the subject.

Nobody around me understood why, neither did I, in fact,
and my reaction upset everybody. I wish I hadn't been so
young during that period, I submitted, I couldn't do anything
else, I was never able to act, you see.

I was shocked when I read *Treblinka**. The author said that
the Jews had allowed themselves to be deported like a flock of
sheep, obedient and stupid. But I didn't feel that and I think
he was mistaken... In fact we simply accepted our fate as
Jews, that's all. And I understand perfectly well why my
parents never tried to hide or change our identity.

My mother often blamed herself for staying with us that
night...

And your father?

Didn't I tell you? My father didn't come back from
deportation. The farewell scene in the train, the separation...
it was final. My mother waited for him in vain; I, however,
knew he wouldn't come back! I still don't understand "why"

---

*In his book on Treblinka (Poland), Jean François Steiner shows how,
at first, the Jews allowed themselves to be arrested, without resisting,
then he retraces the uprising at the camp which was destroyed in 1943.
Treblinka, preface by Simone de Beauvoir, Paris, Fayard 1966.

I did come back. It's really an accident that I'm alive. It's a very uncomfortable feeling. It is my mother who saved me. I was lucky, they never separated me from my mother.

Afterwards, our return to Paris was rather difficult: you can imagine, four women, very much alone, isolated, quite lost, in fact. From the time we came home, or "didn't come home" if you prefer, I was under the impression that it was I who supported my mother! and ever since... it's still the same, sometimes it's such a burden...

I was, obviously, very much behind with my schooling: I was very bright, there was never anybody to advise my mother to let me skip a year, for example.

We never went out. You know, not many people invite a woman on her own with three daughters in tow. We stayed completely shut in, on top of each other; what's more, we didn't have any money, at the end of the month... it distressed me... not my mother!

In my life, except for my daughters, nothing is of vital importance to me. When I see my colleagues fighting out of ambition, I envy them. What's more, I haven't got a competitive nature.

I am neither practising nor a believer. As for my husband, he would have liked a religious wife, or at least someone who cherished the traditions. The Jewish Holidays, I just can't; but because of me, perhaps my daughters won't know enough Jewish history. Maybe, now, it will be possible for me to take more of an interest in Judaism, as I am lucky enough to be Jewish, and be able to benefit from a wealth which has been handed down to us, and which is, apparently, incomparable! Thousands of years of similar experiences...

I'm not well-adjusted, I'm particularly ill at ease in company; I'm always alarmed when someone remembers me, I feel so unimportant! For me, to marry a non-Jew would be unthinkable... and I hope it will be the same for my daughters.

(Suddenly terribly tense) It would be too cruel, wouldn't it, all that... for nothing? I've never been able to demand or ask, deep down, I've never even wanted to! Either things are given to me automatically, or else... Life... it's the same, you see!

***

We are meeting for the first time. You chose to talk in very anonymous surroundings, a café... When I asked you for this interview, you agreed, you simply added: You know I really haven't anything extraordinary to tell you.

In fact, you can see for yourself, I don't know if I've been of any use in your research, but perhaps I had to talk about it once in my lifetime?

A FEW WORDS...

This chapter in the middle of the interviews, it doesn't make sense; normally it should be at the end of the book as a conclusion.

But is there the slightest connection between what is "normal" and the subject being dealt with here? What is more, I shall not try to come to any conclusions: I shall simply underline certain facts which have given separation, reunion, mourning a particular dimension in this situation.

In most cases, the children had to cope with separation not once but several times, and in a climate of agony, fear, sometimes even total panic.

For Madeleine, for Lazare, separation is associated with images of the camp at Pithiviers.

It is when she gets off the coach that Sonia is worried not to see her mother. As soon as he arrived in the unoccupied zone, André asked for his father: his mother told him he was in prison.

Raphaël goes back home, a neighbour joins him, his father asks him to wait for a friend by the roadside.

It is the morning of the great raid. Maurice, his brother, and his mother have taken refuge at an aunt's. The father, who was supposed to join them, never arrives. Worried, his mother and his brother go to the end of the street to look for him. It is only during the evening, when his brother comes back, that Maurice learns of his mother's arrest.

Samuel's father goes out on an errand; he will not come back.

The station platform in Nice, and her young brother whom the Swiss woman will not take with her: this memory is so painful that Hélène has erased it.

Colette, in hiding at a neighbour's, watches her parents and brother getting further and further away, surrounded by French police officers.

It is in the convoy taking them to the camp that Myriam says goodbye to her father.

At the camp of P., Robert is separated from the rest of his family: he is the only one to have a green card. He is told to go away; he wants to go up to his mother to say goodbye; they will not let him, they even strike him because he does not obey quickly enough. His father, who witnesses this scene, powerless to do anything, howls that above all he must not forget that he is Jewish, that he must remain so.

In these interviews, one lament recurs: "I didn't say goodbye."

Then, they were brutally transplanted to an orphanage, a convent, a neighbour's, strangers' homes, to an environment that was completely different from, if not the opposite of the one they were used to. Often to farms, when these children had lived in large towns. Nobody was to know their real identity. Most of them had no news of their relatives, no way of communicating with their parents.

Sometimes, an additional cause for anguish was added to the picture. If they were moved to a different place, seeing as their name was no longer the same, how would their parents know where to find them after the war?

In fact, the child was not always reassured, and they had difficulty establishing relations with their new families. One exception: Joseph, aged five; he was in Switzerland and received visits from his elder sister and his mother.

As soon as France was liberated, they expected life to return to normal: order would be restored. It was a false hope!

Hélène and Louise had been held to ransom; their parents still hadn't come back; after a while, they joined an uncle in Portugal.

Sonia, Colette, Jean were taken in by close relatives, sisters or brothers of their parents.

One of Raphaël's uncles came to fetch him, he took him back to Moissac to the children's home run by his aunt. There, he was reunited with his three year old sister.

In this home, and in many others, they tried to gather together children who were homeless and waiting to meet up with their families: such was Robert's situation.

Madeleine and Joseph knew that their mother had gone back to Paris. Meanwhile they stayed in Switzerland, waiting to be brought home by a special organization.

Lazare went back to Paris with his younger brother and his mother.

Maurice joined his father; he met up with his two sisters; then one brother came back from the *maquis*; the other came back from Buchenwald more than a year later.

André, Paul, Samuel and Paulette's mothers, like so many others were on their own, completely helpless: anxious about the future, the uncertainty as to whether the deported husband would come back, the fact that they had nothing left, jobless, homeless, with no source of income, meant that they could not always take their children back immediately after Liberation. This additional separation was even worse, as the children felt that they were in the way, that they were too heavy a burden for the surviving parent.

The children had to cope with ruptures on several levels; their surroundings, the family and even at school. Many of them had their schooling interrupted for a year, for two years: when they went back, they had fallen a long way behind, they were older than their classmates but they knew less. When you know how much importance Jewish families have always attached to education, you understand why the children felt doubly inadequate and humiliated — they no longer lived up to the image their parents wanted to preserve.

It was hard for them to re-adapt, sometimes it was extremely difficult, almost impossible, they felt they couldn't glue the broken pieces back together again, and what is more, they had the impression that they were alive by mistake.

They had hardly arrived home when another phase began;

that of going backwards and forwards to the Hotel Lutetia, where those who had escaped from the camps were gathered.

Some of the children experienced these hours of waiting: each day they arrived hopeful, only to leave all the more disappointed having witnessed the reunion of other, more fortunate families. They knew what it was to go from one escaped prisoner to another, brandishing photos of a son, a daughter, a brother, a sister, a father, a mother, an uncle, an aunt, a nephew, a niece. Sometimes one of them thought they recognized a face, creating false hopes for those who still refused to acknowledge the facts.

The children who were fortunate enough to go back home found it unrecognizable: one of the parents was missing, the other turned out to be lacking in affection. At home the subject of those who were not there was avoided, and when someone else took their place, the child had no say in the matter.

Nothing was said, nothing was explained: an impression of chaos, of confusion at the heart of these families which had been literally dismembered.

One mother remarried, this time, her brother-in-law, either to respect ancestral traditions or to strengthen the family bond; and the situation proved intolerable.

A child was taken in by one of his parents' brothers or sisters: there was no end to the pain he felt... nothing would heal.

What seemed to be logical was not, what was said went unheard, and what was given could not be accepted.

Motivations were no longer the same, values had changed, words had lost their original meaning, all previous standards had to be revised, everything had to be thought out, conceived anew. People had to find a new way of understanding death, life, and accept their own survival, with all its implications!

To have escaped deportation or to have come back; to lose one parent when others had lost both; to be the sole member of the family to have survived: that is when the feeling of guilt reaches its height. *"I returned to the farm where we had lived together; a criminal always returns to the scene of the crime..."* (Robert).

I feel it is important to underline the fact that in three interviews there are allusions to a schizophrenic sister or son. This confirms the statistics compiled by the Maison Médico-Psychologique Universitaire de Sceaux: over a period of eight years there were twice as many cases of mental illness amongst the Jewish students.

In his autobiography, Jean Daniel writes: "It was easy for me to accept my Jewishness because I never saw my parents humiliated."

At the age when these children experienced separation from their parents, they were in the middle of the identification process, and the search for "new objects", which should have continued its normal course, proved difficult in surroundings which deprived them of their cultural heritage. These children had seen their parents being terrorized, forced to go into hiding or change their names, in short, disappearing completely! The parental image is hardly enhanced, and the child's self-image suffers.

Added to all this are the photos of the deportees in their deliberately "clownish" clothes, in striped pyjamas, with shorn heads, whose hunted, terrified, bewildered looks have nothing human left about them.

All the documents give accounts of the physical and moral torture which reduced them to human wrecks, the constant humiliation they suffered, objects of derision, the sarcasm, the sadism, veritable playthings. With regard to this human material, the notion of value was only raised when it was a question of driving a bargain with certain industrial concerns with a view to experimentation. Seeing them dragging themselves along, exhausted, ordered about with a whip, suffer the most degrading situations without having the strength to rebel, to fight back, is that the image the child must preserve?

That child has had to struggle to salvage even "decent" memories, and the identification process will be even more difficult if it has not been possible to provide a cultural and emotional heritage, and if being Jewish only means one thing:
PERMANENT DANGER OF DEATH.

In fact, there are very few people who know about the circumstances in which their parents perished — some felt the need to find out from archives, to read all the documents available on the subject; others have deliberately avoided everything that evokes their past, they have tried to erase it from their memories. But they often wonder: "Where did they die?" In the sealed convoys? In the camp itself? Were they selected on arrival? Did they die of exhaustion, of cold, of hunger? Were they beaten to death? Did they die in the gas chambers?

"I always said: my father was shot by the Germans. It's a nobler death than the furnaces." (Samuel).

"To be fatherless when you know that your father died naturally is bad enough; in this case it's even worse." (Joseph).

"The furnaces, what were they? Was he burnt like Joan of Arc?" (André).

The mourning of the Jewish child whose parents perished as a result of persecution cannot be compared to the experience of the orphan whose parents died of illness, from an accident, from a natural disaster, through war, bombing or whatever else can nowadays be feared in the domain of "arbitrary death".

The Jewish children have never forgotten that the declared intent of Auschwitz was the total extermination of the Jewish people, which implied their own destruction. That is why they cannot even bring themselves to bury their dead. The imagination refused to dig their own graves, enter the gas chambers, provide fuel for the furnaces. There was no image they could refer to... that was acceptable, for what is still conventionally called human dignity.

They are indeed orphans, but they have also been wounded, ravaged to the core of their beings by a bereavement, the magnitude of which attains atrocious proportions.

It is not hard to understand the feeling of desertion, of anguish which overcomes the child, when he realises that his parents' death has been decided and executed in cold blood by those whose name is also "humanity"!

When the American psychiatrists qualify this tragedy as a

"man-made disaster" they are giving it its true dimension.

In the entire world, why were there so few people who heard the cries of agony, who opposed and fought against the degradation of a race, against their total extermination? Why this refusal to see, to hear? Why that act of abandonment, whether it was deliberate or not?

Yes, why? Why? Why? What, who, is there to cling to in future? If the world allowed that to happen once, why not twice?

This is not intended to be an interrogation, nor even an effort to understand. It is rather the cry of a helpless, abandoned creature who still refuses to accept that the world remains blind and deaf to all his pleas.

In fact, it is more than a cry: it is a howl of revolt, of indignation, of fear, of pain that can no longer be soothed...

I did not want to conclude, I feel that it is better to leave everybody free to pursue their own thoughts. In fact, perhaps it is because I refuse to accept certain conclusions which are unbearable.

Less than thirty five years afterwards: swastikas reappeared; a bomb exploded in a Jewish student dining-hall; a professor at a Paris faculty of medicine openly proclaims his pro-Nazi sympathies in the lecture hall; synagogues and Jewish cemeteries are desecrated; the television series *Holocaust* is held responsible for a new outburst of anti-Semitism; in a Paris lycée, some Jewish children who are being bullied seek protection from their teacher:* "We're afraid..."

So, the word END loses all meaning.

*"Témoignage d'Elisabeth Gille," *Le Monde,* 18 April 1979, p.15.

MAURICE

My recollections of that period... it's hard, they're very hazy.
And yet, to be honest, I was nearly eight.

We lived in rooms that were humble to say the least, in the
XXth *arrondissement** of Paris, and an entire room was
taken up by the sewing machine, the materials that my father
used; he was a tailor, working from home. My mother helped
him, adding the finishing touches by hand. They sewed the
star on to my school pinafore, a big yellow splash on that
black pinafore: the star stood out beautifully. I never felt it
was a humiliation, it was rather a sort of decoration that I was
the only one in the class to wear.

The other children never called me a "dirty Jew". I was
fortunate enough not to have had to face that problem,
perhaps because I was top of my class at that time.

My eldest brother was twenty-one in 1941; he was a photographer's errand boy. One morning, he was caught in an identity inspection raid – he was released an hour later. And so, he
said nothing, neither to his employer, nor to our parents, and
he went straight off on his bicycle. Two hours later, he was
caught in another raid, they didn't let him go again.

He was sent to Drancy in March 1941, and then deported
to Buchenwald and then he was taken to another camp, I
don't remember which one...

Then there were only three children left at home with my

*district

parents, as one of my sisters, who was ill, was put into an institution.

The morning of the great raid, in July 1942, two inspectors came round very early to warn us that they would be back to fetch us in an hour.

My mother, my brother, my sister and myself hurriedly left to go to an aunt's house, four hundred yards away. She was not yet threatened by the laws, as her husband was a prisoner of war.

As for my father, he went down to the *Familistère*, a little grocer's shop that was just below our flat. Why there? I wonder. Perhaps it was necessary to disperse the family. In any case, he was supposed to join us as soon as possible at my aunt's.

More than an hour later, he still hadn't arrived. My mother, who was very worried, then decided to go along and find out what was happening there, and, so that nobody would recognize her, she borrowed a coat and a headscarf from my aunt. Taking my brother with her, she went towards our house, walking on the opposite side of the street. That is when the *concierge** recognized her: the police were coming out of the building, she pointed out my mother and my brother. They both began to run, they wanted to get away. My brother was twenty, he escaped, my mother didn't.

That evening my father and my brother joined us, separately. It must have been my brother who told us what had happened to my mother.

I think I knew about it the same evening; and yet I don't remember exactly. I know, however, that I didn't cry at that point; I cried later, at supper, over the spinach which I didn't like.

In the suburbs, my father managed to find a family who agreed to hide him; another was going to look after me.

My two sisters were both in hiding in an institution, my brother had joined the *maquis*.

My father had to earn enough to pay the two families and

*caretaker

the institution for the two girls, even though he wasn't allowed to work. The people who were hiding him arranged to go to Paris twice a week, to call into a clothes shop. They collected work for my father and took it back when it was finished.

In my new family, I didn't wear the star; they were the only people who knew I was Jewish. But, however, I kept my name, which didn't sound at all foreign.

I went to primary school, I had pals. Best of all, I saw my father twice a week.

I can't tell you anything about my stay in that family... time passed, that's all.

You see, compared with other children, I was extraordinarily lucky; I didn't feel distressed because my father wasn't far away.

Obviously, I had no news of my mother, nor of my eldest brother, but as I didn't know what deportation was, I waited. I don't think I asked my father any questions about them, if he had heard from them he would have told me, so...

At the end of 1943, the family who were looking after me became frightened; I had to move again. Worst of all, I ended up staying with fervent Pétain followers. They agreed to look after a child, with all the risks that involved, as, in spite of their support for Pétain, they were against arresting Jewish children. I didn't feel at ease in their house, the situation was really too difficult.

As soon as France was liberated, my father and I went back to Paris. We hadn't been able to get our rooms back. We rented others in the same building, on the floor below, and we waited.

My brother came back from the *maquis*, my sisters from the institution. And then my eldest brother came back from deportation, in April 1945. I wasn't at the Hotel Lutetia when he arrived.

Little by little, without ever speaking about it, we gave up hope as far as my mother was concerned, the waiting was over.

My brothers and sisters got married very quickly, my

father and I were left, just the two of us.

You know, I am convinced that the events we lived through as children can happen again, at any time. For me, everything in life has remained relative, and I have the impression that the "human drama" is something I experience daily.

Fortunately I must have a highly perfected defence mechanism. Furthermore, when I saw the Auschwitz camp on television, the showers where my mother was probably gassed, I didn't superimpose any images, especially not...

***

We have known each other for more than ten years.

At one time we saw each other fairly often.

But it was his wife who said, one day, "Perhaps he'll agree to talk about it".

I hadn't thought of asking him for this interview, as he had never even hinted that his mother died when he was a child.

RAPHAËL

At the end of 1941, my father, my mother and I are still in Paris. I wear the star; I remember, I was sitting near my mother when she sewed it on to my coat, she sang while she was sewing and she said: "How lucky you are, my son! Do you know that few children are entitled to wear this star?"

Every recreation the children would bully me, the teachers looked on without intervening, I went home beaten up (I was small, that didn't help matters), but I had a pal, a real friend, I met up with him again after the war. He came to my defence; he couldn't bear those sessions of "all against one" as he called them, even though he was only eight.

A child comes to your defence, an adult stands there with his arms folded. You don't forget that!

I had the impression that I was fighting for a just cause. I was singled out in a way, according to my mother's explanations. Only, I hadn't chosen to be singled out... I had to accept it!

My mother was pregnant. The raids were more and more frequent. My father was a member of the first Resistance networks in Paris. He sends us away, my mother and myself, with the help of the railway workers;* they hid us in the belly

* Right from the beginning of the war, the railway workers took initiatives in resisting the Germans. Not only did they organize sabotages, but they were responsible for helping people to cross over to the unoccupied zone, for helping those who escaped, and for the delivery of letters thrown from the trains by the deportees.

of an engine. That was how we crossed the demarcation line. It was horrific, that journey.

We breathed with great difficulty, sparks flew everywhere, they had told us, "Even if the Germans bang, play dead." What a fateful expression...

The Germans came. I could see their boots through the tiny air-slit. My mother began to perspire profusely. I was afraid, especially for her, she had to stay put in that minute hiding place!

Finally the railway workers got us out of there; we arrived at Moissac. That was where almost four hundred young Jews were gathered, without their parents.† That home was shelter; my father's sister ran it; we celebrated the Jewish holidays there, we were scouts, life carried on. Then, danger. We must hurriedly disperse and the young people must be hidden on farms, in the *maquis*.

My father is in the *maquis*: he comes back from time to time, he leaves messages in the handlebars of my bicycle, I must never look at them. "Scout's honour", I never did look, in fact, I'm simply afraid when I use the bike.

One day, I'm cycling home, a neighbour joins me: "Your father says that you mustn't go home any more, you are to wait for a friend of his, here".

So, while waiting by the roadside, we settle down to a game of cards on the bank, we play *belote*. The friend arrives, takes me away with him, a long way from Moissac: I don't ask why, nor do I ask where my parents and my little sister (who was born in Moissac), are. I stayed with him until France was liberated.

Then an uncle comes to fetch me. I return to Mossaic. You know the 'Moissac Citadel' was quite something. If you read

---

† In June 1940, the Jewish *Eclaireurs* (scouts) chose Moissac (in the Tarn and Garonne region) as one of the evacuation centres. They set up rural groups, carpentry workshops, ironwork, sewing facilities. Their organization was disbanded in 1943, (as was the UGIF), by Darquier de Pellepoix, the Commissioner for Jewish Affairs. In August 1943, the scouts joined the *Organisation Juive de Combat*, in the Tarn area *maquis*.

a book called *La Résistance Juive**, you'll see what Moissac stood for.

My father and my mother had been arrested on the same day by the Germans; when they arrived, my father escaped through the window, but he was injured. He was a member of the Resistance, so was my mother. It was she who destroyed the list. She saved many lives, but she paid with her own life, as she died at Auschwitz.

They had been in the same convoy. In the train that took them towards Auschwitz, my mother was cold. My father put his lumber-jacket around her and she tied a scarf round her head. As soon as she arrived, she was selected. She was only thirty seven, but, bundled up like that, she seemed older.

She was awarded the *Croix de Guerre* posthumously. I'm very proud of her, but I would have preferred her to be alive.

My father came back from Auschwitz alone. He didn't open his mouth, he no longer laughed, no longer spoke to anyone: I was frightened of him, I didn't recognize him any more!

My sister was three when my father took us back to Paris.

You see, the most difficult period of my life was after my father's return... and my mother's "non-return"... it was hard!

My father would wake up at night in the grip of terrifying nightmares; he would howl, he was covered in sweat. And so, I would go to him, sponge his face, talk to him... I was frightened myself.

When I learned that he had been made to join Dr Mengele's famous team,† I understood his howling. Now, it is less frequent but it still occurs.

---

* Anny Latour, *La Résistance Juive, 1940 – 1944*, Paris, Stock, 1970., pp. 36 – 39. See "Landmarks" 15 August 1940, summer 1942.

† Head doctor at Auschwitz from May 1943 until the end. Nicknamed "The Angel of Death" by the prisoners, he "selected" the deportees on their arrival at the camp, sending those who were incapable of doing heavy work straight to the gas chambers. The archetype of the S.S. doctors, he indulged in the most monstrous experiments, the remote objective of which was to perfect a superior race, destined to replace the inferior races like the Jews and the Gypsies after their extermination.

He has never laughed since, he has never spoken a kind word to me, he doubtless felt it was a heavy burden bringing up my sister and myself.

He has never wanted to bring another woman into the house.

Mealtimes were disastrous, he'd be behind his newspaper, not a word would be exchanged, and that... has been going on since...

My sister isn't with us any more... she has been having treatment for a long time... schizophrenia.

You see, whereas I had my mother until I was nine, she, on the other hand, has no recollection of her. It is I who replaced both her father and her mother until she was seventeen. It was hard. And all that only to end up like this. What a disaster!

I had the impression, you see, that I was in the way. How can I explain? My father resented my existence, that's what I felt. So I did everything I could to make him accept me, it was subconscious, I understood that later.

You see, if I'd had to choose, I think I'd have chosen my father's life, with deportation and everything, but not to have paid for it with my life, since 1944... his deportation and perhaps his return, without my mother!

He came back hard, inflexible. Success was the only thing that mattered, and to achieve it he battled fiercely, even against me.

He broke me, he made me into his thing.

I had to prove to myself that I could live without him, and he wouldn't allow me to: every girl I introduced to him he demolished in two sentences. And I gave in.

I haven't got the guts to hurt him, in any way... even to save my life! On the other hand, it's as though he's trying to avenge himself on me... but for what? For whom?

He suffered a lot from being humiliated in deportation, it's the humiliation which appears to have been most unbearable for him... and he often tries to humiliate me, his son.

It was impossible, I didn't understand at all.

One day, I read in an American magazine that the aggressiveness of the deportees was cruelly felt by their children. What rot! And my sister who'll never get over it... I really love my father. I'm all he's got left; I know how much I matter to him, but I also know he is no longer capable of living a normal life. He never got over his deportation... neither did we!

You are the only person I could talk to about it.

***

Raphaël is one of my best friends, and has been for more than twenty years. It is he who urged me to publish this book. "The world must know", he said, "how we have been marked by this deportation, as far as the third generation. It is horrible... I didn't have a youth, I no longer have a mother, I have a sister who needs treatment, a father who hasn't been able to lead a normal life since he came back. An entire existence ruined, a total waste!"

SONIA

Yesterday afternoon I agreed to talk to you and, a little while later, I was panic-stricken at the idea of what I was going to be able to tell you.

I feel as though my childhood is a total blank, to such an extent that I am deeply perturbed by it.

Then I felt the need to see my brother, to tell him that I was going to talk about the past, I even asked him if he could help me remember something. But perhaps he has no recollection either; through never talking about it, perhaps it's only natural to forget?

I remember a ceremony with an Orthodox priest, a parish priest to baptize us, my brother and myself, before we left for boarding school.

Before we went away, my mother took us to a hairdresser's to have our hair cut as short as possible. For fear of lice. The hairdresser picked up the clippers and shaved my brother's head, I could no longer recognize him, he was bald as a coot. Like all little girls of Russian origin, I wore two long plaits. The hairdresser was becoming irritated, he couldn't find the scissors for me. I think that it was done with my mother's consent; he picked up the clippers again, I came out with my head shaved!

We arrived at this boarding school, about ten kilometres north of Nice; I have no memories whatsoever of this period. Perhaps I was too young?

That was in 1944, I was born in 1937, I was seven. And yet,

I remember one episode during recreation; I was sitting on a bench, the children were laughing at me and my shaved head; I suffered a great deal because of it.

Why did my mother agree to let them crop my hair? One day I asked my aunt Véronique, my father's sister who is still alive; she replied that my mother was a bad mother, there was no other reason... And on that point, whether on my father's side or on my mother's side, they all agree that she was a bad mother.

I can remember arguments, violent arguments between my parents. My father was seventeen years older than my mother, it was his third marriage.

My mother must have had love affairs: but in particular, she was very flighty, refusing to behave, and even to dress, like everyone else.

She didn't love me as much as my brother, she had wanted to have him; but I don't think I mattered very much to her, and yet, the more they tell me she was a bad mother, the more they describe her absurd qualities, the more I am drawn to her as time goes by, I think I understand her. I wish I could have known her. That bad mother, who, every Sunday, cycled for two or three hours to come and see my brother and me!

One morning, a telegram arrived at the boarding school; "Father very ill". They immediately put us on the next bus to Nice. I simply can't remember who came to meet us when we arrived. My mother? My father? Or Aunt Véronique? It's really odd, I can't think who it was. On the other hand, I do remember there was a real party as soon as we got home. My father wasn't ill. Why that telegram? Why the party? I don't think I asked any questions. It was only after the war that I found out the reason for the telegram: my father had been arrested, and we were celebrating because they had released him.

It was the following day, I think, that I heard my parents discussing us. My mother wanted to send us straight back to boarding school; my father was against it; they both envisaged the possibility that they might be sent to special camps in France; but should they keep the children? My father felt we would be safer with them. He tried to persuade my mother that with the sense of organization, the reputed cleanliness of the Germans, the living conditions, the hygiene would surely be perfectly acceptable, even for young children. My mother had her way; the next day, we went back to boarding school.

So, a short time afterwards, when the same telegram arrived again, my brother and I took the bus once more, delighted. No doubt there would be festivities again, perhaps we would leave the boarding school for good?

When the bus arrived, it was Irène, our cousin, who was waiting for us, with a friend whom she introduced to us as Louis.

Irène had nothing to be afraid of, her mother's second husband who was a captain in the French army, was a prisoner of war in Germany; she had adopted her mother's new name.

Irène and Louis were sixteen or seventeen; they laughed, told us stories; they took charge of us from the moment we got off the bus, and took us straight to a school in Nice, where we stayed for eight to ten days. I don't think my brother and I asked a single question about our parents, nor did we ask why they had brought us back to send us to a different school.

At the beginning of the war, we lived in a big house in Nice, where I still live with my children. There were my parents, my brother, my Aunt Véronique, her son and myself.

My cousin had joined the *maquis* from the beginning. My brother and I were boarders. So, when they came to arrest the family, there were only my parents and my Aunt Véronique, my father's sister.

In Nice itself, before leaving for Drancy, my aunt poisoned herself. She had to be taken to hospital, that's what saved her. With the co-operation of the hospital staff (who gave her injections to induce a high temperature) her departure was postponed – that was in April 1944 – then she stayed in Nice; she was saved thanks to Pastor E., a pastor who helped the Jews, and who used to visit that hospital. My aunt took him into her confidence. (It was his son, Louis, who had come to meet us when we got off the bus.) Later, that pastor became our guardian.

In May 1944, my Aunt Tania, my mother's sister and Irène's mother, took us to an estate not far from Nice. There were a great many young people, in particular there was Louis's brother and a friend of his. They made a cheerful group.

But I have very unhappy memories of my stay there. I was sad, very sad. I felt lonely, disoriented, not at all at ease. I often cried, over trifles, at times when no-one was expecting me to. Everything upset me; in fact I was suffering, but I was incapable of expressing or understanding it.

I had simply been told that my parents had gone on a long journey abroad. I never talked about them, not even to my brother. I think I was already waiting, I don't know. In any case, I took it very badly when my Aunt Tania's husband came back from Germany where he had been a prisoner of war.

My cousin took over the knitting factory my parents had set up before the war: my brother and I took the road to the *Lycée*.

Even if we never talked about it, we waited, we hoped.

One day, coming home from school, my brother noticed that the shutters of our house were wide open. Without another word, we ran, convinced that our parents were there, that they had come back, that they were waiting for us. We arrived so breathless, and there was nothing; it was simply our imagination.

It's like thinking you've recognized someone, it's awful. You run after a woman in the street, thinking she's your mother, and then she turns round and everything collapses. How many times have I been a victim of that!

Meanwhile, a happy event; my cousin got married; his wife was very kind to us. And then, a few years later, they both died, he of a very rare illness, on his return from a mountain climbing expedition in Peru; and she a short while afterwards, during an ascent in the Himalayas; she was called "the highest woman in the world".

For my Aunt Véronique, that was very hard.

My parents were both of Russian origin; at home we spoke

Russian, never Yiddish. What's more, I don't remember any religious practice.

They felt they were Russian, not Jewish. And I had the same reaction. It was impossible for me to accept my Jewishness, yes, really impossible! Moreover, it is not very long since I have accepted it, one or two years at the most.

I have never mixed with Jewish people, I married a non-Jew; I got divorced, I was thirty-four, the age at which my mother died.

My thirty-fourth year was a disaster; I spent a crazy year, absolutely crazy, I didn't understand what was happening to me, I even had a breakdown, without there being any real reason; nobody around me understood what was going on; I gave in. I had reactions I could no longer control, I behaved against my better judgement, it was awful.

Since then I have thought that it must have been very difficult for me to live beyond what my mother had experienced.

One day, at the house of some friends, I met a man whom I found very attractive. I was prepared to see him again, when I learned his surname: it was a Jewish name. I never saw him again! I couldn't: it was like incest!

A friend, who wanted to please me, offered me a trip to Israel. I didn't want to hurt his feelings; I didn't dare refuse, but I wondered: why to Israel? I'd have preferred to have gone somewhere else; in spite of myself I was aware of a past there.

And then I saw *Fiddler on the Roof*. My father used to play the violin, my mother accompanied him on the piano. My eldest daughter first held a violin at the age of three; she is studying dentistry, but she still plays the violin. I used to play the piano; I had reached a very high standard, non-professional; I studied under Lucette Descaves when I came to Paris. I still play, sometimes I accompany my daughter.

That's my parents' legacy, they left me the idea that doing well at school was much less important than practising my scales regularly!

I realised that my parents' disappearance was permanent thanks to the Klarsfields' book.* When I saw, under the date

of 29th April 1944, my parents' names, what a shock! Thirty
five years later! It took me thirty five years to admit, finally...
You know, I kept hoping for so long! In January 1945, my
father was still alive, so...

My brother is two years older than I am, he rarely talks
about the past. He was brilliant at school and at university,
with as natural a gift for maths as for philosophy. He opposed
the teaching system. Accumulating all the possible
administrative "offences", he managed to get himself sacked
from the *Education Nationale*.

He lives in a garret, with the toilet on the landing; he's a
painter, tiler, depending on whatever turns up, and he has
lived like this for years.

Since 1968, he has been living with a non-Jewish woman,
from a totally different background and culture. She accepts
him as he is, never asks any questions about his past; she
knows she mustn't.

She found out by chance, from a friend of his, that his
parents died in deportation.

I love my brother very much, he matters a great deal to me; I
even have the feeling that it is he who has given me the things
that have most affected me.

Age has completely changed him, physically: he has become
the spitting image of the Jewish tailor of Vilno, it's
astonishing. He's an ascetic; he completely rejects the
consumer society, he doesn't want to benefit from it. I'm
rather proud of him myself.

When I take stock of my life, it's not very positive. I live
mainly for others, I'm always available, in the end I get
swallowed up!

I studied psychology, not without good reason: but before
that I studied arts; I ran a building society. In fact, I have never
met with failure in my professional life, but that is not the most
important thing. I feel I have more or less missed out on my
life as a woman.

On the other hand, in my relationship with my two

* See end of "Landmarks".

daughters, I feel something very deep, very real.

And yet, I have not always been a good mother either. When they were very young, I sent them to clubs, to holiday camps, I did everything I could to make then independent as early as possible, as if I was already preparing for an eventual separation. And when I saw that they said goodbye without worrying in the slightest, I was very happy.

For four years a friend of my youngest daughter's has been living with us. She is of Russian origin.

I think she feels completely at home, she pinches my clothes like the other two, and if something I do displeases her, she lets me know just as vehemently.

A friend reproached me for not having brought up my daughters in a Jewish atmosphere. "They won't have any roots," he said.

But how can I pass on to them what I didn't receive myself?

JEAN

My mother was Hungarian. My father, a Czech, was a foreman in a little factory in the north of France. He drove a shuttle train from the factory to a depot. Half way there was a house: he never failed to hoot twice when he went past. Then I would run out to the little engine, climb in beside my father and we would set off again together...

I can no longer picture my father, perhaps I can remember my mother's face better...?

I can remember the mezuzah* above their door, and a Jewish holiday when we swung a chicken above our heads... what is it called? I think it was the Day of Atonement! There were Hebrew books at home: I don't remember anything else...

October 1943: I'm a boarder in the first year at a school in a nearby town. I wear the star: every recreation, the other children call me names, beat me up. I am very young but I do well in class. I wait impatiently for the end of that first week; I'm going to tell my parents what it's like here, and they'll take me away.

On the Saturday, at lunchtime, I wait by the roadside for my father who is to come and fetch me in the van belonging to the factory. At that moment some Germans arrive, they get out of two cars and come into the school.

*A small metal scroll, containing a prayer, which Jews fix to the door-frame.

A pupil says: "Great, they're going to requisition the school, we won't be able to come back..." I am delighted at the idea. I don't have time to reply; the headmaster arrives, breathless, he calls me: "Leave your belongings here, young man, take to your heels and run in the direction of the forest, as far and as quickly as you can, whatever you do, don't stop." I do as he tells me, I don't understand anything... Evening falls, I'm still in the neighbouring forest, I'm hungry, tired and cold. I decide to make my way home on foot.

I hide in the woods as soon as I hear a car or a motorbike... but I catch sight of the village vet on a motorbike; I call him. He's been looking for me since the early afternoon (I presume now that he was a member of the Resistance, and that the headmaster had informed him). I climb on to the bike. Just in time, the German patrols overtake us in their cars.

It is on the bike that he tells me: "Your parents have been taken away by the Germans; your sister hasn't, but we haven't been able to find her since... She must have been at school when it happened, no-one knows what has become of her." I don't cry but I begin to shiver, and my teeth start chattering. I must add that it was cold on the back of the bike...

He cannot keep me with him, it's too dangerous. Have I anybody to go to? Then I remember that, the previous week, my mother had been to visit some people who didn't wear the star: she had insisted on taking my sister and myself with her. After a while I finally found their house; we are there, I'm exhausted, my teeth are chattering. We ring the bell. They open the door and all but slam it in our faces!

Fortunately the vet persists, but they scold me, they tell me that I'll get them arrested... my sister had already arrived there, on her bicycle.

We can't stay with them. The vet tells us not to worry, he'll come back and get us, tomorrow he'll have found a solution. The people agree to let us stay overnight.

I can't eat anything, nor can my sister: but at least we are together again!

That evening, my sister cries and tells me that when they

came to arrest my parents, she was cycling home from school; my mother simply told her to ask the neighbour to look after the chickens... and my sister understood from the expression in my mother's eyes what that meant. It took her such a long time to find these people's house...

We have an aunt in Vendôme, the wife of my father's brother. She's a Catholic, surely she'll look after us! That same evening, we write to her.

The next day, we are sent to a farm, they are good people; they have promised to look after us until our aunt comes for us. We are called Rousseau.

She never came, although we wrote two more letters.

And so, the farmers advised us to set out for Vendôme. My sister and I left together, and we crossed the demarcation line. At last we arrived in Vendôme: "Oh, it's them!" Those are the words my aunt greeted us with... I never dared ask whether or not she had received our letters.

My sister and I were famished... she fed us, gave us a place to sleep, but we understood, we weren't exactly welcome!

My aunt has an only daughter, she cooks little delicacies for her. We eat at the same table, but there are no little delicacies for us!

Mind you, I don't blame my aunt, she loved her daughter, and I must admit that we never went hungry.

She made life hard for us though. To such an extent, that one day, my sister couldn't take any more, she ran away. Two days later, fortunately, they found her.

But I didn't answer back, I put up with everything. One scene has stayed in my mind; she hit me with a tea-towel, in front of my school mates, because my chair hadn't been properly put back in its place at the table. I don't think I deserved that, did I? I... I can no longer judge.

One day, a letter came to my aunt's house from my parents: but she refused to show it to us. "Destination Auschwitz", was all she said to us. The letter had been thrown from the train, picked up by the railway workers' Resistance network.

The Church became my refuge. I began to pray for my parents to come back as soon as possible. It never crossed my mind that they wouldn't come back, no, I never imagined anything like that. But I promised God that if they came back soon, I would convert. Had they come back, I should no doubt have become a fervent Catholic!

When France was liberated, I waited, I waited for a long time, with no results. I never saw my parents again, I wasn't even able to say goodbye to them!

My uncle told me one day that there was no longer any hope that they would come back, so we would have to envisage one solution for my sister, and another for me: they couldn't afford to bring both of us up.

For my sister the answer was straightforward: they had contacted a distant cousin of my mother's, in the United States, who had agreed to give her a home.

As for me, I had applied for a grant. I came first in the examination: they were sending me to boarding school in the next town. I would stay with them for one month a year, during the summer holidays, never during the rest of the year, because my aunt was too tired... I agreed joyfully... I would study... and if, in spite of what they said, my parents came back, they would go straight to my uncle, they would be able to find me easily then.

I was shattered at the idea of being separated from my sister. I was obsessed with the fear that I would never see her again, like my parents. Her departure was terrible for me (years later, a friend of mine was going to the United States; I asked him to look my sister up. He married her, they came back to live in France. Over there, she had been spoilt, she had great difficulty adjusting).

Boarding school was tougher than I expected. Not from the work point of view: I had very good marks; there was no virtue in that, all I could do was study, so... But I learned the meaning of loneliness. It was hard, I was the only full-time boarder.

In fact, I felt alone as soon as I understood that my parents wouldn't be coming back!

After six months, I make friends with a boy whose parents go and see the headmaster to ask him to allow me to spend a

Sunday with them. The headmaster agrees.

And from the first year to the upper-sixth form, I spent every weekend with them, all the short holidays, and part of the summer holidays. I felt almost at home in their house. I owe them everything.

My uncle always refused to let me become a war orphan. I still don't know why. Therefore I couldn't benefit from the allowances granted to war orphans, in particular for higher education. I was penniless. I worked during the day, I studied in the evenings, during the period that preceded the entrance examination for the *Ecole Normale d'Instituteurs.* *

At the *Ecole Normale* I had acquaintances, pals: I could never make friends, I was afraid of people.

Then I was given a post as primary school teacher. It's a profession that I still love. My wife is a primary school teacher, she's nine years younger than I am. I didn't want to get married, I was afraid... of my fiancée's reactions when I had to admit: "I'm Jewish". She took it very well; she simply insisted I convert to Catholicism before we got married.

But why do I agree to everything?

I am godfather to the son of a friend of mine who openly preaches his anti-Semitism! He doesn't know I'm Jewish. If he knew, I wonder how he'd react!

I realize that I've done everything I could to make a new start in life. I had to erase everything, to write off the past. I even thought I had succeeded. Apart from the nightmares. My wife wakes me up, I sob out loud, apparently. I don't remember anything, but these nightmares leave me terribly distressed. My wife has never asked any questions about them.

And when I dream that my parents come back... I wake up by myself, unhappy because it's only a dream, and the following day is miserable.

I'd like to eat once again, just once, the cakes my mother used to make, they were Hungarian cakes, with walnuts... For years, I saved walnuts, for their return; and sometimes,

---

* Primary teachers' training school.

automatically, I still put walnuts in my pocket.

My mother was very gentle and indulgent with us...

For twenty years I've been suffering from haemorrhagic rectocolitis. I was told to consult a psychologist, or a psychiatrist: I did, but I couldn't face up to the real problem. I waited for them to guess what it was, to meet me half-way, I couldn't be the first to bring it up; a year ago, it was you who asked me if I was Jewish! I wonder how I managed not to talk about it for thirty five years. As if everything were conspiring against me, the pupils I became friendly with were often Jewish...

Two years ago, on holiday, I bumped into one of my pupils; his parents invited us to join them; they're Jewish, most of their friends are too, and I felt at ease. When I came back, I was so pleased with that holiday that I went and thanked them for having accepted me into their group. And this year we're going away with them again.

I am used to being rejected; I'm not used to being accepted. To be welcome as well, it was so surprising; Jews who didn't guess my origins welcomed me with open arms!

My parents: I haven't rejected them, but deep down, I'm still afraid of one thing: being Jewish causes so much unhappiness! If my parents hadn't been Jewish, they wouldn't have been deported, I would have lived like other children, so I didn't want to be Jewish any more!

I waited for them for such a long time when I was a child, I often imagined our reunion! I can't help it, when I see a form that reminds me of my father or my mother, I want to hope for stupid things: they were captured by the Russians, they've just arrived in France, they're looking for me. I have never wanted to alter my name in any way for this reason: so that they will be able to find me, if, by chance...

I often wonder why I don't know how to enjoy life! If I had been able to forget the past completely, perhaps I could have lived normally, perhaps I'd have been content with what I have, and no longer think about what I don't have any more.

I don't have any photos of my parents, I don't have their last letter: I don't have a grave to visit. Just one document:

Believed dead... Auschwitz 1943. It's hard.

You know, I'm afraid of the violence I sometimes feel within me, I have the impression I'm a rebel for life. And, oddly, I feel I don't have the right to be alive!

HELENE AND LOUISE: TWO SISTERS
I. Hélène

I was born in 1938 in Paris, I was the eldest of three children; my sister Louise, born in 1939; my younger brother was born in May 1943.

My parents, my maternal grandparents and my younger brother were deported to Auschwitz. None of them returned.

Of Paris, I remember nothing. Of Nice, where we must have spent nearly a year, I can recall one incident: I asked the whole family to sit on the big divan and lift their feet off the ground. They gave in to my request, everybody laughed, they wondered why; I had the impression that they were on the water and that nothing could happen that way... In July 1942, a Swiss woman, a friend of my uncle's, arrived in Nice. She came to fetch my sister and myself, to go on a journey. I don't remember leaving, and I don't remember the journey; in the evening we arrived in Paris, we went to her house.

The following day my sister and I are immediately separated. I am sent to a convent. I was only given one piece of advice: never to speak Yiddish again, and... forget that I am Jewish. Besides, the mother superior wants to convert me; I don't want to convert, I offer resistance, she tells me about the devil. I am frightened and I howl every night, I wake the whole dormitory. I don't want to be a Catholic, or rather, I don't want to be transformed, and apparently the devil can do that at night when I'm asleep. It's horrible. Up till my marriage, I had nightmares about that devil!

The Swiss woman comes back, she puts me in a family

where I'm with my sister again. This is in Chateau-Thierry; the farmers are good people, and I go to school.

France is liberated. Nobody comes to fetch us. I'm worried. I never talk about it. Louise is too young, she isn't aware of anything. One evening I overhear the farmers talking. They are still receiving money for our board, but they no longer understand what's happening.

Eight months later, the Swiss woman comes to fetch us: I never ask a single question about my parents... I subsequently found out that we were the subject of ignominious dealings: the Swiss woman contacted my uncle, who had taken refuge in Portugal, she was the only person who knew our new names and where she had hidden us! He had to pay a lot of money, he almost blamed us, subconsciously. All the same, he negotiated for eight months before paying up!

I've often thought about it. I think that parents pay straightaway to see their children again... I don't hold it against him, it's my uncle who saved us, throughout the war it was he who paid the Swiss woman the money for our keep. And afterwards he brought us up.

The Swiss woman sends us to Portugal. For two years life is like a dream... The woman who lives with my uncle is wonderful, but one day, disaster: they have an argument and my uncle is left alone with us. For him, it's impossible! He sends us to Paris, to my mother's sister. She had come back from deportation. That is the period in my life when I suffered most. Only her daughter mattered, she had taken us in because my uncle paid her generously! She's my mother's sister. I hate her, I constantly think that God is unjust: why didn't my mother come back, when my aunt had been saved?

Fortunately my uncle and his girlfriend have made up their quarrel, they take us back straightaway. My uncle's wife can't do enough for me, we're friends.

It's not the same with my sister.

I found out on the same day, in 1969, that the woman I called "my aunt", my uncle's wife, was suffering from a malignant tumour, and that I was pregnant with my third child. I hoped it would be a girl and that she would take after my aunt.

Fortunately, all my wishes were fulfilled. Spiritually, this daughter is my aunt!

When my aunt died, I was in despair, I had the impression I was losing my mother for the second time; and when my uncle died, a short while afterwards, I felt that my entire family had died out for good.

My nights were full of terror, I had nightmares. One in particular, that I still have, but not so often over the last few years: *I learn that it is possible to trace my parents. I travel, I travel, alone to this place, I finally reach it... It's a desert, nothing lives there, nothing grows there, and all of a sudden, I catch sight of three round sort of holes, one small one and two larger ones... They have hidden themselves there to survive, it's certain. Then I rush over and lift with difficulty the stone covering the opening of the holes... I call them, I tell them that it's me, Hélène, their daughter, I clear the stone out of the way, I look in. There is a heap of bones and a mocking voice laughs. Then, I scream and... I wake up.*

You know I've never asked other people any questions. I couldn't talk about it, the words got stuck in the back of my throat. But I said to myself: If at least my mother comes back, even ill... but let her come back... I hoped for a long time!

I've never been able to talk about... all that. If an allusion is made to the deportation in my hearing... I run away, it's cowardly, but I don't want to break down in front of other people.

My husband is Jewish, but he's from North Africa. He is cheerful, he didn't experience anything of all that, he hasn't got those problems.

I've never spoken Yiddish again; and I insisted that my children learn German to... understand Yiddish... that beats all, doesn't it?

You know, I didn't say goodbye to my parents, I had no idea what our leaving Nice signified. I learned afterwards that they were caught in the raid two days later...

But they were aware of the danger, they saved us, they

stayed behind... and they showed nothing; I must have left as if for a pleasure trip...

Their only consolation must surely have been the fact that they had succeeded in saving us! But... what I'm saying is absolutely disgraceful... was it necessary to save us at all costs, for us to live afterwards without parents, with the impression of always being abandoned...

My God, I haven't the right to think that... My brother, on the other hand, wasn't so fortunate... How horrible! Why us... and not him? My son is called after my brother!

HELENE AND LOUISE
II. Louise

My sister and I were already in the train with the Swiss woman. The train was about to leave. My mother begged that woman to take my little eighteen month old brother too. She refused. The train moved off, my mother was holding the child out towards the door...

I can't see my parents' faces. All I have are photos... but after all they could be photos of anyone, I wouldn't be able to tell the difference!

In the first family of farmers, I slept next to a little boy, he was younger than me. He coughed a lot, he coughed up blood. He died in his sleep. I was the one who noticed that he no longer stirred. I wasn't afraid, they wouldn't let me go to the funeral, I saw it from the window. Then I was with my sister again, in another family, without incident...

My sister understands everything, she tries to admit... I don't. Beneath my calm exterior, I'm constantly rebellious... it doesn't take much: as though I'm perpetually poised between anger and tears. I force myself not to be miserable if I can help it, otherwise life is impossible.

I don't have happy memories of the Swiss woman, cold as a fish, hypocritical. Why didn't she want to save my brother? Such a young child, it isn't easy, but all the same, it was a question of his life. She didn't even have the excuse of not knowing, my mother did tell her that my brother's life depended on her! My parents had therefore foreseen...

You know, they were arrested the following day. It was the

great raid of Nice. . .

I've never forgiven my mother's sister for the way she behaved towards my sister and myself. I hated that woman. I must say she did everything to make us hate her: she treated us like two Cinderellas, only her daughter mattered. Not even my sister could succeed in getting herself accepted. I found that totally unjust: why her? Why did she come back from deportation and not my mother? What's more, I wondered anxiously, how much she resembled my mother, whom I couldn't remember at all.

Subsequently I was very pleased not to look like my elder sister. I could argue to myself that it was possible that my mother was completely different from her sister! I have a strange feeling of having been abandoned, especially as my uncle told me one day that when my mother was pregnant with me, she didn't want to keep me; she was undecided for a long time and she had given in to the entreaties of her elder brother. As if, added my uncle, I owed him my life twice over, before my birth and afterwards, as it's he who provided for us, even during the war, without our knowing.

But one thing reassured me: everybody loves my sister, and so, my mother loved her, that's certain; in spite of that she left my sister in the same way as she left me. . . and she wanted to let my younger brother go too. It's very hard, in fact, to live with the feeling that. . . perhaps it was a way of getting rid of me. . . and to have to reassure myself constantly by thinking: "Of course not, she wanted to save me. . ."

Only the reality consoles me because in fact, my mother did save me! My uncle loved me, that I knew. . . but I didn't want my uncle and his girlfriend to take my parents' place!

My sister got herself accepted by everybody, she was loved by the people round her, it reassured her, that was her way of surviving. Whereas I was the opposite. I didn't want to be pitied because I was an orphan, above all, I didn't want them to think that my parents could be replaced. And so I violently rejected anyone who tried to do so. . . and at the same time, they rejected me, you see. But for me, it was a means of survival, that's all.

With my husband, I've never had that attitude however, I'm happy that he values me.

I have three children, I know they love me. I have no doubts about that. They are the only ones I am sure of!

The most awful thing is: I blame my parents for having left us. It took this interview for me to admit it to myself finally! Especially my mother: I found out much later that my uncle had sent us visas so that we could get out of France, in 1941; at that time it was possible, we had just arrived in Nice.

But my grandparents, who were very old, didn't want to leave their country yet again. And my mother didn't want to leave her parents on their own in France. I can't help thinking that her parents mattered more to her... than we did!

She did her duty as a daughter – there's no doubt about that – she sacrificed her life for them... and ours, because I am not happy, I'm not happy, even if I have every reason to be!

When the Germans came to arrest them, my mother left a parcel with the *concierge* asking her to keep it until a member of the family came to get it. In that parcel were her jewels, the unused visas, and a few photos.

My husband is a photographer. Photography is of vital importance to me. I told you, my sister at least has her memories; but I have nothing!

I'm not religious, I can't believe in God, I'm too much of a rebel... and I have the acute feeling that I haven't the right to rebel... because I was saved, I wasn't deported... I've had a gilt-edged existence compared to others, compared to my brother...

I insisted however on my son's having his *Bar Mitzvah.* Try and explain that!

That way it seemed that... my parents, my brother hadn't "died for nothing". Because if they died for nothing, I no longer understand why I am alive...

***

Louise was really worried about this interview being published. but she couldn't put her finger on what it was that troubled her, when suddenly, she exclaimed: "I don't want to be anonymous any more, I've had enough, I can't bear it any more. Use this interview, but publish it under my real name: Louise Brodsky!"

COLETTE

I had parents, I had two elder brothers, they were all deported to Auschwitz, none of them came back. I am the only survivor.

My parents fought so that I could live, they bought my life, they paid for it, it's the truth...

I wore the star, but what I remember is an incident with my father: the first time he sewed it on his coat, he sewed French decorations that he had received during the First World War all round it. When he went down into the street, the neighbours congratulated him, a stranger even got off his bicycle to shake his hand; my father was very moved by this.

At the beginning of 1941, my elder brother, Jacques, crossed over to the unoccupied zone, we thought that he was the only one in danger.

I don't know why my parents decided to register as Jews, but I remember they discussed it for an entire evening.

I must add that they were both born in France; French was their native tongue; they were very much integrated; I don't know if they spoke Yiddish, and I don't remember them observing any religious practices.

For them, it was essential to keep within the law. If they were always law-abiding, they couldn't be accused of anything. Before the War, my father was an ironmonger's assistant; during the War he got hold of a sewing machine, and to make a living, he mended clothes. In 1943 my parents became afraid for my safety, they sent me to a convent as a boarder. I no longer wore the star, the nuns simply asked me never to say that I was Jewish. It was my first time away from my family, especially from my mother.

I was unhappy, my mother would come to see me once a week, when she left, it was distressing.

Then my parents took me back. I have no idea why, perhaps they thought I would be safer with them, perhaps they felt I was too unhappy at boarding school? I simply slept every night at a neighbour's house.

Now, it was morning when the French police came to arrest the family. My brother, Michel, was unlucky. He was leaving for work, he was late, they arrested him on the pavement just as he was coming out of the house; he was wearing the star, they asked him if he was really the son, he went back in with them.

When the French inspectors arrived, my mother asked me to stay quietly in another room. I was ten, I heard my parents bargaining to save me. My mother begged them, then she offered them our few belongings; they took the money, the jewels and agreed to take me down to our neighbour's flat. On the staircase, one of the inspectors warned me that if ever I breathed a word about what had happened, my parents would be hurt.

I am sure that my parents also tried to buy my brother's life, but he was already sixteen, it was no longer possible.

On the other hand, for their own lives, that's a different story! When the police took them away, I was at the neighbour's, I was watching through the window. My mother looked up at me, and very discreetly, she made a sign, that's all.

I still see that scene over and over again.

That same evening, the neighbour took me to one of my aunts. Her husband had already been arrested, she lived alone with her two sons aged eight and ten. What was she going to do with me?

She had the idea of sending me back to the nuns. They were taking the whole orphanage on holiday for two months; I went away with them.

My memories of that holiday are painful; solitude,

unhappiness; I was constantly ill at ease, in spite of the nuns' kindness. I lived with the uncertainty of my future; for the first time I felt I was being "given a home".

When France was liberated, I went back to my aunt's. We both thought it was a temporary arrangement, it didn't occur to us that nobody would return. You see, my parents were deported in June 1944, among the very last convoys, and my brothers were young, strong...

As for my elder brother, his deportation was even more maddening. In the unoccupied zone he had tuberculous peritonitis and had to be hospitalized in a sanatorium, at Font-Romeu.

The neighbour who took me in had a son who had been my brother's best friend for years, they had the same first name, but was my brother aware that he belonged to the young *Doriotistes?** In any case, this young Doriotist went on a journey to the Pyrenees. How he got hold of my brother's address, I have no idea. Perhaps they wrote to each other, perhaps my parents wished to have first-hand news.

Anyhow, he went to visit him. During this visit, my brother even introduced another Jewish boy to him, a convalescent.

An argument broke out between my brother and his childhood friend. They parted angry at each other, but my brother would never have imagined that his friend would betray him. Two days later, they came to arrest my brother and his Jewish companion. My brother left the sanatorium on a stretcher. That is what I was told afterwards.

At my aunt's, we listened to the lists of survivors on the radio every day. My aunt went to the Hotel Lutetia alone; she showed people the photos of her husband, her sister, her brother-in-law, her two nephews!

We had one slight hope, people thought they had seen my brother, Michel, alive in February 1945. But how can you be

---

* Doriotistes: members or sympathizers of the Parti Populaire Française, founded in 1936, by Jacques Doriot. An extreme right-wing Hitlerite movement.

sure of recognizing a face from a photo? He must have changed so...

I always felt great admiration for my elder brother, Jacques. He was brilliant, a sportsman, a musician; he was planning to study fine arts; he had everything.

When I was waiting for them to come back from deportation, I remember, however, that I hoped for the return of the second oldest brother. Perhaps because I didn't want to seem too demanding: I asked for the person I was least attached to, to come back.

I waited a long time, especially for that brother.

From the age of eleven till I was sixteen, I lived with my aunt and two cousins. Her husband didn't come back either; she had very little income and three children to take care of. In spite of all her good will, I felt I wasn't her daughter and no doubt I held it against her.

After the School Certificate, my aunt gave me the choice: either I could become a boarder at school as a war orphan, (she wouldn't have to pay a penny) or I could leave school and earn my own living.

I don't have a grudge against her, I know how difficult it was for her to bring up the three of us, but all the same, when it was a question of her own sons a few years later, she didn't make them face that choice.

But I wouldn't hear of boarding school, not after the convent. And so, while I was an au pair girl in England, I took a correspondence course, and passed my matriculation without any difficulty.

I told one of my aunts, who accused me of being obstinate, temperamental, that I missed my mother's cuddles. In fact it's my mother I missed, and still do.

I was ten when they were deported; I think it's my mother's absence that has marked me most, even more than the deportation.

If I did well at school, if I worked desperately hard for my *agrégation,** I have always had the impression it was so that she could be proud of me.

When I met my future husband, I think the fact that he was

studying fine arts had something to do with my being attracted to him. Now I have four children, my eldest son is called after my eldest brother.

My husband isn't Jewish. Our children are atheists, like us, but they know they are half Jewish. To be Jewish, I wonder what meaning that can hold for me! To not dare break away from the past?

I feel that I have struggled so much during my life, and now I don't even understand the meaning of that struggle. It's as though there is an immense vacuum around me, a vacuum, which, in spite of all my efforts, I cannot fill.

Even my relationship with my children is difficult, though I should so much have liked to be successful in that area, especially. It's really very hard to live, yes, it's really very hard.

* Agrégation: a competitive examination for admission to state teaching posts.

ROBERT

I was born in 1929. The eldest of four children, I am the sole survivor.

I was brought up in a rigidly orthodox home. I rebelled against the religious obligations; one evening, I even refused to say my prayers, I can still remember the punishment I was given.

One thing strikes me: why didn't Jews who were as poor and as religious as my parents were, live in the ghetto? Perhaps because the "interior" had always been important to my parents: there were two children to a bedroom, the house sparkled with cleanliness, I think my parents refused the filth and the promiscuity of the ghetto.

From Alsace we were sent to Royan; then, in 1941, all the Jews were put under house-arrest in Dordogne. There we were allocated to a few old farms that had been requisitioned by the State. There too, my father had managed to obtain a farm for just ourselves, while many other Jewish families were trying, on the contrary, to stick together.

My mother took care of the interior, my father and I of the farm; within a short time, my father proved to be such a good farmer (he who had been a door-to-door clothes salesman before), that the neighbouring farmers were jealous. Those were the happiest years of my life.

My father and I loved working the land.

We would have been happy, the four of us, but the yellow star was a constant reminder that we weren't simple country folk, like the others.

That star, I felt it as a terrible humiliation: I refused to wear it, my parents made me, they told me there was to be no argument about it.

At school, at almost every recreation, a gang of country children would pick on me, we beat each other up, it was hard, I had no-one to defend me, that is perhaps when I began to feel very lonely. Fortunately I was big and strong for my age, that was a great help. And then, after a few months, they got tired of it, I even had a pal.

I had two aunts that I was very fond of: my mother's youngest sisters. They lived together ten kilometres away from our farm. At the beginning of 1942, they were taken to Drancy.

So, tell me, why did we stay there? We were four kilometres from the demarcation line, I used to fetch the milk every day, close by. I told myself that it would be easy through the forest. It didn't even seem to occur to my parents.

One evening some gendarmes arrived. They asked us to get ready, to take only a small bundle each, above all nothing cumbersome. They said that they would come back for us in three hours.

I remember that my mother cried, so did I, as we prepared our bundles. They even sent me to ask a neighbour to look after the chickens while we were away. Then we waited by the roadside, clutching our bundles, so as not to be late. We got on to the bus which stopped to pick up all the Jewish families. Not one was missing! When I think about it, it makes me sick.

The arrival at A. There were many buses... the children declared as French must hold a green slip of paper (I still don't understand why I was declared as French, and my brothers and sisters who were much younger, were not). We are separated from our parents, from our brothers and sisters: children howled, parents cried, there were awful scenes.

My father took advantage of the hubbub to come up to me, he gives me all the family's money: 700 francs (which I've always kept), his penknife, their wedding rings, their watches, a ring of my mother's, and above all an address that I must keep safely, that of our former Rabbi, who has taken refuge in P. If I don't know where to go, if I have any problems, I'll know who to turn to.

A man comes up to me, he entrusts me with his six year old son: "Don't ever leave him," he begs me, "he is so young, I'm putting him in your hands, he's called Bernard Bercovitz."

A little boy who was lovingly holding a gilt-edged book then walked over to me and said: "keep it". It was surely his most precious possession. He must have been eight or nine. He gave me Perrault's *Contes*.

In the midst of this nightmare, I want to say goodbye to my mother, they won't let me go near her, a German orders me to leave, I don't obey quickly enough, he hits me!

My father watches this scene, helpless, and suddenly he cries: "Robert, never forget you are Jewish and you must remain Jewish!" Those were his last words, I can hear them as if it were yesterday. He didn't say: "I love you, don't be afraid, take care of yourself," but he said that single sentence...

They call the register, they count us: there are twenty of us; I am the eldest, I am thirteen, the age of manhood.

A parish priest comes to fetch us, we walk for ages, the youngest ones can't go on any more, they cry incessantly, they ask for their parents; this priest doesn't say a word to us during the entire journey.

At last we arrive at a home, juvenile delinquents or welfare cases, I don't know. We stay there for a few days. Nobody looks after us; we eat, we sleep. The twenty of us together, we don't mix with the others, nobody asks us to.

I ask the priest if he can find out where my parents are. His replies are very evasive.

After four days, the priest assembles all the children, Jewish and non-Jewish, and he tells us that we're going to a very beautiful house.

The house is large, spacious, light, well-equipped, but there, the priest asks the Jewish children to attend mass, like the others, and talks of our becoming Christians. In fact, he's already busy converting us.

But I refuse to attend mass; the priest punishes me; I stand my ground, and... I prevent little Bernard from going, for his father has entrusted him to me, and I feel responsible.

One day, I receive an unsealed letter, it's from Drancy, it's a letter from my parents. My father scolds me: "What kind of son are you then? We left you all that we had, we sent you the parcel vouchers, for your brothers and sister are very hungry, you are the only person who hasn't sent anything." I see red, I rush to the priest, "where are my parents' letters, what have you done with the parcel vouchers?" I am out of my mind, "my parents think I've forgotten them, do you realise?" I cry, stamp my feet, I have a fit of hysterics... He answers, more than embarrassed, that they've sent parcels on my behalf, and he shows me a label on the envelope, *No use sending letters or parcels, left for unknown destination.*

I fall ill the next day, I remember nothing of that period, I had violent jaundice. I recover. The religious pressure grows stronger and stronger: it becomes unbearable: but I know I "must remain a Jew". And so, in secret, I manage to post a letter to the Rabbi whose address I've kept. I tell him they're trying to convert us.

Three days later, a woman arrives; the Rabbi has sent her to fetch the twenty children. The Rabbi welcomes us, and the same day allocates us to families... Jewish, who wear the star, just like us. Tell me, where were his brains, that Rabbi? When I think about it, it's worse than Kafka!

In the family I'm staying with, I have to share a room with a boy of seven who is an only child, and who doesn't want me around: he totally rejects me; his parents can't make him see reason. I'm as unhappy as can be: it is the most miserable period of my life. I am alone and rejected by another child; a Jew like myself, but who has his parents. One morning he goes as far as saying that he has peed on my toothbrush. It's the last straw.

I write to the Rabbi again, I beg him to find me another family. He deals with it immediately, and I am sent to another Jewish family, tradespeople. The husband has been deported; the wife is very ill; it's the maid who looks after me; I am with a fifteen year old girl, Judith, who has been sent there for the same reason.

It's heaven. I fall in love with Judith; I work desperately hard at school, I want to skip a year, I feel capable of it; the maid spoils us, I am alive again, everything seems possible!

Bernard is with a family not far from mine, we go to school together.

I can recall one incident; the children wearing the star are not allowed to cross the Main Square, they must go round it. But in the middle of this Square there are roundabouts... and children riding on them. Bernard and I, on our way home from school, are leaning against a window, watching. A woman then comes out of the baker's, she's holding a little boy by the hand. He's eating a cake. Perhaps the look on our faces is eloquent? She goes back into the shop, comes out again, quickly thrusts a box at us, and walks off. The box is full of cakes!

Then I leave Bernard standing there holding the box, I run in search of the woman. Above all, I don't want her to think we are "Jewish and badly brought up". I catch up with her, I look at her, "Thank you, thank you very much!" And, bright red, I go off to eat the cakes.

One morning, a summons arrives at the house where we are staying: *All French Jewish children must be assembled, and leave the families they are living with.* Once again, a bus takes us away; we are "spilled out" at the P. concentration camp.

Bernard, Judith and I arrive there amongst the first; for hours the buses follow each other in rapid succession, full of children of all ages. I can't even say how many there were of us, they were swarming all over the place, and not a single adult with us.

That evening, they brought us great basins of water and cabbage leaves – I almost forgot, one piece of bread each.

On the third day, we received a barrel of sweets from the Red Cross. The sweets, which were unwrapped, were stuck together, the children were killing each other to get at them.

I ended up in the barrel, I can still picture myself in there!

Twice a day, the basins of cabbage arrived, and for almost a week, we stayed there, without any adults being present, you can't imagine what it was like.

We played, played till we dropped from exhaustion, we needed to!

One morning, they finally put us all on a train, laid on specially for us; the whole train was full of children, we were coming back to Paris. From there, we were sent to different centres.

I want to stay with Judith and Bernard. It's impossible, I'm fourteen, I must go to a work centre for Jewish boys aged between fourteen and twenty.

We are taken care of by the UGIF, a Jewish organization under German control. It's terrible.

Bernard, Judith and all the other children were deported during the months that followed. Bernard died at Auschwitz; only six of them came back, among them, Judith. I didn't succeed in protecting Bernard, I still feel responsible for him now!

In the work centre, I'm the youngest, I learn carpentry, but above all, I learn how to "survive", to fight so that nobody takes what's on my plate.

One day, the Resistance warns the director of the camp that there's going to be a raid. The director says nothing, but a teacher warns us, he tells us to leave the centre for the day. But go where?

A pal and I go to another Jewish centre on foot, then we come back, there wasn't a raid that day.

One morning I receive a letter: "My dear Robert, I am a friend of your parents. My name won't mean anything to you. I have something for you. Meet me etc..."

I decide to go. They are expecting me. That's when I recognize the doctor from the centre, he explains that my name has been listed among others by a Resistance network. They want to save us, in spite of the director, who doesn't want to do anything. (They used the same strategy with the others). The raid is to take place that evening. He'll procure false papers for me. I trust him... I was one of the last Jewish teenagers to be saved by Dr M.'s network.

I change my name, I no longer wear the star, that makes me feel better, my name is François.

I live with a primary school teacher at le Raincy. She's very nice, she doesn't ask for more than I can give! I am to stay with her for the duration of my secondary education: after taking my matriculation, I have to live in the student residence-hall; as a war orphan, the State is responsible for me.

I start studying medicine. When I enrol at Medical School, a tall, gregarious lad enrols at the same time, we end up next to each other for laboratory work. A few months later he suggests I move in with him, he lives nearby, it will be more convenient than the student residence. I arrive early.

It's his mother who opens the door: while we are waiting for him we chat, she has a very gentle air, she asks me where my family is. Feeling reassured, I say a few words: P., in 1943? We were there too, she says.

It's incredible, but true; I've found the cake-lady. The gregarious lad is the boy whose hand she was holding.

The son returns, then the father. Everyone is moved by this encounter.

I must consider myself as their second son.

That's how I lived with them until I got married: I'm their second child, really.

Talking of family, a funny thing happened to me: when I passed my matric, the schoolteacher at le Raincy asked me what I'd like as a present. I told her: "a journey home, but alone."

It was a long time after the war. That journey was distressing, everybody had advised me against it, but I had to go. I saw our house again, then I found my parent's best friends' house. Their name was painted on the door afresh. I ring the bell... nobody; it was early on a Sunday afternoon.

And so, while I am waiting, I walk around and look at all the names painted on the doors of the other houses. Perhaps I'll find other friends of my parents? I scrutinize the names, and all of a sudden, my name, the spelling of which is rather unusual, and I am even certain that I recognize my father's handwriting (the name is written by hand). I'm going crazy; I

ring the bell, nobody. And in the five minutes that follow, I am
seized by a terrible anger, an impossible rage! They came
back, they live without me, they didn't look for me, it isn't
impossible... or they went about it as stupidly as they went
about avoiding deportation... A wild anger rises in me, I'm
going to tell them what I think, I've been looking for them
since 1945; they are monstrous! I choke.

Without noticing, in a daze, I'm back in front of their
friends' house. I ring the bell again. They are at home. I greet
them, I ask them:

"How long have my parents been back? Why didn't they
find me?"

They look at me as if I am mad.

"But your parents and your entire family died in
deportation..."

"We didn't even think you were alive either!"

"But don't you understand? I'm telling you my parents are
alive, they live in the new district, close by...!"

Then they sit me down, they treat me like a child who needs
calming.

And I tell them what I've seen.

"It's true," they say, "that name exists, that man is a lawyer,
his name is spelt like yours; we know him, he's from Alsace, he
isn't Jewish..."

Then I leave abruptly, and I go straight to the Synagogue. I
see my parents' names on a commemorative tablet, my
brothers', my sister's and... my own, along with all the others
who had been deported from the town. And I must say that it
didn't seem that strange. For, after all, am I alive?

In fact, I don't know what it is to live. I live in the past, and,
worst of all, when I hear children say that their parents were
wonderful, it hurts, because I don't even have that
consolation.

I blame them, do you understand? Yes, I blame the dead,
who paid for my life with their own! It's unbearable! They did
nothing for their own survival. Nothing! Nothing!

(*Robert has taken his head in his hands, he hides his face.*)

They really went to the slaughterhouse like sheep. And they

left me, the only one of the family; and I had to survive, at all costs.

You know, sometimes I would glimpse someone that reminded me of my father, and in spite of myself, I would follow or run after him, and not so long ago either.

I haven't any photos of my mother. I've forgotten her face. I have a photo of my father.

I returned to Dordogne twice, with my wife and daughters. As you know, "a criminal always returns to the scene of the crime," doesn't he?

Criminal?

Yes, I said criminal, it's odd... but after all, they're dead and I'm alive.

I wanted to buy, at all costs, the farm where we lived together; the owner wouldn't agree to sell.

When I came back to Paris, I had a strange dream, which put a stop to years of nightmares: *I was walking in front of the farm, there were five holes, (each in the shape of one of those water towers that I had actually seen, on that trip, and which had been dug recently), two big, round holes, three little ones. I had at last discovered where they were buried... and for wonder, on the farm where we were so happy!*

My eldest daughter, who is a student, is going to live in Israel, for good. She told me she had to do what I hadn't accomplished... a full circle has been completed... the torch has been handed down...

(*All of a sudden, very weary*): My father would have been proud of her, whereas I'm glad she's an atheist like me, but capable of fully accepting her Jewishness! I often wonder how I'd react if she married a non-Jew... it would hurt me a lot, no doubt, and yet... I wouldn't oppose it.

(*After two minutes of silence, he adds with a huge smile*): But I know she wouldn't do that!

You see, I survived with a lot of luck, but I didn't just stand there with my arms folded...

What a nightmare all that! I don't remember if I told you: from the train that took them to Auschwitz, my mother dropped a card; it reached me, when I was ill, at the priests' home. There were just a few words: "Boubele" (a Yiddish endearment), "look after yourself. We are on our way to Auschwitz. I love you, Mummy."

She no longer mentioned the parcels... It was fortunate that I received that message, otherwise I wouldn't have fought to survive...

AFTERWORD
BY BRUNO BETTELHEIM

The terrible silence of children who are coerced to endure more than they can bear! The mute agonies they suffer when they are forced to bury deep in their souls an injury, an anguish that never leaves them, a grief so severe that it defies expression! And this not just when the destructive event happened, or during its immediate aftermath, not only in childhood, when we all find it difficult to put into words, to open up about what concerns us most intensely, about which we feel most deeply, but for years on end. It is a hurt so painful, so omnipresent, so all encompassing, that it seems impossible to talk about it even a lifetime later. Only it is not a lifetime later for those who still suffer from it; it is as present, as real as it was when it happened.

What had been inflicted in childhood on those who speak in these pages was so devastating, so destructive to their very existence, that they can not talk about it, not even to those closest to them. As Paul says: "I've never talked about it, not even to my wife, and especially not to my mother." The reason they can not, do not want to speak about it is not so much the wish to avoid thinking about the facts, because thinking about them is too painful. They do not need to recall the facts; they never forgot them. These facts have stayed with them all the time, have haunted them all their lives. In any case, these facts are familiar to all who know them, are no secret to the world at large; on the contrary, they are well known, even if some wish to forget them because they arouse their guilt feelings.

The unwillingness to talk on the part of those whom Claudine Vegh interviewed is only partly due to their conviction that no words are commensurate to convey what has happened to them. I believe that among the deeper reasons for their reluctance to talk about themselves, about how what had been done to them in childhood had ruined their lives, is their awareness that those to whom they might talk about it all would want them to accept, to make their peace with what had happened to them; and this they know they can not do. Also others might believe they understand the victim's agonies after they have listened to him talk about them, while he knows that by comprehending the facts they know nothing about the all pervasive nature of his sufferings. So why talk about it to others? This is why they can open up only to a person such as Claudine Vegh, since they expect her to understand them from her own experience, which paralleled theirs. And even to her they can talk at first only with greatest hesitation.

It is the feelings which their losses, their deprivations, have left them with which are so overwhelming that they threaten to engulf them, to tear down the dams they erected against becoming flooded by their sorrows. These dams they had to construct in order to be able to engage in the difficult task of creating a life for themselves after the devastation they had experienced. It was strenuous work, and the results are at best tenuous, still it was the only way they could survive, and they do not want to see the results of their efforts threatened. To be able to build some kind of life for themselves, they had to hide their feelings so deeply within the innermost recesses of their minds that they themselves can hardly reach them.

In order to be able to go on with living, first by doing well in school, by passing examinations, by entering a profession, and later by getting married, having children, trying to do justice to the obligations to their families, they had to repress these feelings so deeply that all they are aware of is how terribly difficult life is for them, and how empty. Colette knows well this emptiness, although she tried to escape it by doubting whether there is any sense in her being Jewish, when her husband is not, and when their four children are brought up without any religion. "I feel that I have struggled so hard during my life, and now I don't even understand the meaning of that struggle. It's as though there is an immense void round me, a void which, in spite of all my efforts, I cannot fill.".... "It's really very hard to live, yes, it's really very hard."

All whom Claudine Vegh sought out knew that talking with her about their past would arouse feelings too difficult to bear; this is why they dreaded the interview. "I was panic-stricken at the idea of what I was going to be able to tell you" says Sonia. She, too, fears the emptiness she feels: "I feel as though my childhood is a total blank, to such an extent that I am deeply perturbed by it." Paulette begins "You know, I agreed to do this interview, but I'm scared... very scared."

And this although nearly thirty-five years have passed since the events they are about to recall. A lifetime of normal living, of having grown up and having found a place in life, of having established a home of their own, of having children, should by then have healed these ancient wounds. Only these are not old wounds, long scarred over; on the contrary, they have never healed, and as soon as touched begin to bleed all over again. Only it is not a normal life that these former child victims are now living, however much it may seem that to all outer appearances.

This is why Claudine Vegh introduces her profoundly moving story and the equally affecting reports of her fellow victims with telling about an event she attended which normally should have been a most happy occasion: the *Bar Mitzvah* of a friend of her daughter. Contrary to the pride and happy feelings one would expect a mother to experience on the festive celebration of her son's gaining adult status – at least in religious terms – the mother of this boy covered her face with her hands, withdrew into herself and, as the ceremony reached its climax, cried. Another mother who also attended the celebration of the boy's *Bar Mitzvah*, bewildered by his mother's unhappiness on such a happy occasion, remarked about it to Claudine Vegh. This vividly brought to her mind her feelings when, just a year ago, her son had celebrated his religious reaching of manhood in the same synagogue. Then she, too, had experienced great pain.

It made her keenly aware that normally happy events are not that for those who had been so severely crippled in childhood that, in consequence, the important occurrences in their lives take on dimensions very different for those which are considered normal. Because of their past experiences, anxieties cut more deeply as they tend to attach themselves to terrible childhood traumata and revive their memory. With it they take on much more devastating aspects than they would in those who have not been so early and so destructively bereaved. What would be happy events under normal circumstances make these unfortunate victims of childhood disaster feel only more keenly the irreplaceable losses they had experienced. Normal happiness eludes them because what to others would be a happy event tends to revive memories of how their childhood had been deprived of all happiness; it makes them recall only more acutely their losses. As Charles remarks, "I don't know what happiness is, but then I never have done..." Or, more to the point, for Lazare, "It is in moments of happiness that it is terrible." Despite Louise's quiet and composed appearance, she know that in reality "I'm perpetually poised between anger and tears."

It seems that it easily requires twenty or more years to gain sufficient distance to realize how differently one experiences life because of the particular tragedy suffered in childhood. As Paul Friedländer writes in *Quand vient le souvenir...* "It was only at this time in my life, when I was around thirty, that I realized how much the past molded my vision of things, how much the essential appeared to me through a particular prism that could never be eliminated."[1] It was Claudine Vegh's realization of that prism through which she saw the events of the Bar Mitzvah, of how different were the emotions aroused in her by this event from those which are accepted as normal, which suddenly convinced her to drop the writing of the usual type of memoire required for becoming a psychiatrist, although she had been working on it for some six months. She decided to engage in a very different, much more important investigation which would elucidate the nature of the particular prism through which she and her fellow child victims viewed themselves and the world.

Although I do not know the reasons which motivated her discarding of the originally planned study in favour of the present one, it makes sense as preparation for becoming a psychiatrist. To be able to help others with the difficulties they encounter in living , one must know what made one the person one is, be aware in which respects one's views of things differ from those whom one is going to treat; good reason to explore how one's life history has conditioned one's perspectives. But much more is involved in this study than research required for becoming a psychiatrist.

The much more general and much greater significance of these interviews is the exploration of one of the great tragedies of our time, and of its lasting consequences for the victims. This required investigating how others who had suffered like her managed, or managed only barely to go through life. Claudine Vegh might also have been motivated by a desire to finally unburden herself, might have dimly felt that only as others like her unburdened themselves might she be able to do the same, as she indeed does in this important book.

We owe her gratitude for the courage with which she undertook a most difficult and painful task, because her account opens a window on experiences we need to acknowledge, understand, and most of all have compassion for if we want to live in peace with ourselves. In more or less distant ways we all who have lived through the world of the round-ups, the deportations, and the concentration and extermination camps have been part of what has happened to the children at that time, however far removed we personally were from what took place then. Its aftermath continues to make its imprint felt in the world in which we live.

Why were the child victims unable to talk about what happened to them, why is it still so terribly difficult for them twenty or thirty years later to speak about what had happened to them when they were children? And why is it so important that these matters are talked about? I believe these two questions are closely related, because what cannot be talked about can also not be put to rest; and if it is not, the wounds continue to fester from generation to generation, because, to quote Raphaël, "The world must know how we have been marked by this deportation, through to the third generation. It's horrible..."

If there should be any doubt that these horrible events continue to mark the next generation, a book recently published in the United States dispels it.[2] Helen Epstein's parents were both survivors of the German extermination camps. Her life has been marked and marred by her parents' fate, and by their inability to talk about it. And this although she herself was born and raised in the United States. Unlike those who speak in this book, Helen Epstein had never been dragged away from her home, had never been forcibly separated from her parents, or in order to save her life, never had to hide from anybody. Her parents made extraordinary efforts to raise their children so that they would feel themselves secure, as they indeed were, living in New York. Helen Epstein, as a child of survivors of the extermination camps, nevertheless felt herself terribly burdened by her parents' past, and by what it did to them in the present. Grown up, she wanted to find out whether her fate was unique, or whether it was similar to others who were born to parents like hers. So she sought them out and talked with them. They, like her, had been raised in comparative safety. Still, she found them all affected by their parents' past ordeals, although each in some different way. They had suffered from their parents' inability to open up about their experiences and about what these had done to them.

Helen Epstein describes the consequences of the unspoken misery of her parents by means of the image of having had to construct an iron box that she carried deeply buried within herself. This box made her life miserable: "For years it lay in an iron box buried so deep inside me that I was never sure just what it was. I knew I carried slippery, combustible things more secret than sex and more dangerous than any shadow or ghost. Ghosts had shape and name. What lay inside my iron box had none. Whatever lived inside me was so potent that words crumbled before they could describe it."

But is it the inability to name, to describe what oppresses one which forces one to bury things so deep within oneself that they can no longer be reached, and being unreachable seem to have an existence of their own which eats away one's life, one's right to be oneself, to enjoy things, even the right to live? Jean wonders "I often wonder why I don't know how to enjoy life." What he fears is locked up and buried in his "iron box" are feelings of violence. "You know, I'm afraid of the violence I sometimes feel within me, I have the impression I'm a rebel for life. And, oddly, I feel I don't have the right to be alive!" If one fears that on opening up what is buried deep within oneself one may find that one has no right to live, then it is clear why one does not dare to look at what it is that one cannot face.

Friedländer writes: "It took me a long, long time to find the way back to my own past. I could not banish the memory of events themselves, but if I tried to speak of them or pick up a pen to describe them, I immediately found myself in the grip of a strange paralysis."[3]

What is the cause of this paralysis? Why could those with whom Claudine Vegh spoke not understand why she would want to talk about their losses, their bereavements? Why this wall of silence which they had erected as soon as they experienced the loss of their parents? An unwillingness to talk about it which in little Claudine Rozengard's case found its first expression in her telling her parents: "Go quickly, go quickly, I'm staying." I believe the reason for it was only partly anxiety about her parents' safety. The little girl would not have so readily decided to remain with her foster parents if she had feared she might see her parents never again; if she had thought that, she would have insisted on remaining with them. She hurried them on to go in order to cut as short as possible a separation which completely overwhelmed her. If she had allowed herself time to give in to her feelings, to say good-bye to her parents, she could not have separated herself from them. By not permitting oneself time to think and to feel, one could separate oneself from one's parents by maintaining to oneself that this was only a temporary separation.

When, on the lucky return of her mother, she learned that her father had died, her reaction was equally immediate "Let's never talk about it again." A decision which she carried to the extreme: "And, for more than twenty years, I was never able to pronounce the words 'daddy' or 'father', nor could I bear to hear any allusion to that period of my childhood." This was not the attitude of one single child; on the contrary, it was the general reaction of the children who had lost their parents. Indeed: "What a strange world it was, where children never spoke of their parents, of their families, of their homes... never to 'talk about it' was one of the rules of the camp, a rule that nobody ever enforced! Sadness, a child's grief or tears, were felt by everybody, myself included, to be unacceptable." Why this repression of feelings, this denial of obvious facts of the greatest importance, of the most far reaching consequences?

After all, at other times, as a result of other cataclysmic events, children have lost their parents in the past more often during periods of starvation, or due to the devastation of wars. It happens even in modern times in earthquakes or floods. These children suffer grievously, but they feel no inability to talk about what had happened; they can speak about their parents, and how terribly they miss them. In short, the children can mourn their parents, and by mourning them openly can slowly make their peace with their fate and hence do not feel they have no right to live when their parents had perished.

I believe part of the particular tragedy of those whom Claudine Vegh speaks about is that fate prevented them from mourning their parents, and this is why the by now old wounds have failed to heal.

Of course, at first there was no reason to mourn; the hope was that the parents would return. The children tried to cling to this hope as long as possible. When Sonia tells "I don't think my brother and I asked a single question about our parents, nor did we ask why they had brought us back to send us to a different school," it seems clear that the children were afraid to hear the truth. In order to be able to hang on to their hopes, they preferred not to ask any questions, not to mention the subject. So Sonia says, "I never talked about it, not even with my brother." And she knows why neither she nor her brother ever talked about what was at all times foremost in their minds: "Even if we never talked about, we waited, we hoped." As long as one did not talk about it, it was not quite true, and one did not need to give up all hope. When Claudine, like the others, for some twenty years never mentioned her father, nor allowed any reference to be made to him, this was only partly to protect herself against being overwhelmed by feelings so unmanageable that she would not have been able to go on with the ordinary task of life. I believe that the deeper, more powerful reason was that she, like the others, in her subconscious held on to the belief that the parent was not gone forever, that by some miracle he might return. André reveals the unconscious connection between his not talking about the lost father and keeping him alive within himself when he says: "I never speak of my father to anyone, he is within me, that is all, that is enough." For the same reason Robert believes many years later that his parents have returned, and when he says "In fact, I don't know what it is to live," he reveals that he does not know what it means to live in the present, because "I live in the past." His real life is in the past when his parents were still alive.

Even under normal circumstances when hope wears thin for the return of a close family member who has disappeared, it is very difficult to stop hoping and to accept that he has perished. Unless some clearly incontrovertible physical evidence of a parent's death has been found, those who loved him are unwilling to give up hope, and do not accept some report that he has died. Our desire to believe that it cannot have happened, that it can not be true is so strong that greater certainty is required before we can force ourselves to accept the most painful news. And if this is so under normal circumstances, Claudine Vegh reminds us, "Is there the remotest connection between what is 'normal' and the subject being dealt with here?"

But the impossibility of giving up hope was not the only reason why the child victims could not accept their parents' death, why they still cannot make their peace with it, nor why they are still haunted by what happened so long ago as if it had happened only yesterday.

After a bereavement, in order to be able to go on with the business of living, one must first have mourned one's loss. Mourning the death of a parent is a very demanding, complex and difficult psychological process, requiring for a time all one's concentration, all one's inner resources, all one's energy. It is a task to which one must devote, at least for a few days, all one's faculties; particularly until, and right after the funeral, but also for some time afterwards. Only if one does this can one slowly master the task of mourning, and with it, slow step by slow step, return to active living despite the bereavement, and regain one's interest in life.

This difficult work of mourning is made a bit easier if we can prepare ourselves for it. For example, when one can slowly withdraw one's emotions from the person who is about to die, while at the same time in some measure take part in his dying. If so, one can say one's good-byes while he is still alive, can take part, so to speak, in his making his transition from life to death. If this is not possible, it helps when at least one can take leave from his body, see the corpse, participate in the burial, take part in the funeral rites. All this helps to convince that – against all one's desires – one has to accept the fact that this person has died.

Even then it is nearly impossible to master all the psychological demands involved in first mourning, and then in returning to living, unless one is helped in doing so by others and by appropriate rituals. We need most of all the support of those to whom we are most deeply attached, normally the members of our closest family. We need them to rally around us, to share our grief; be it in the Jewish form of sitting shivah, that of an Irish wake, or whatever other form the rallying of relatives and friends around the bereaved takes in other ethnic groups. The presence and support of all these people restores our hope that not all is lost, that there are still significant others left to live with and for. Even the respect of relative strangers for the difficult process of mourning which we have to undergo helps, their expressions of compassion, even the respect they show the passing hearse. It is not the dead person who needs that respect be shown to his corpse, it is the survivors who need it. Even that is not enough; we need to be supported in the work of mourning by the rituals religion and society have created for this purpose. That is why since earliest times burial rituals were among the most important and elaborate religious ceremonies.

There is no point in going into any details of what is involved in mourning here. Only a very few aspects of mourning were mentioned to show how difficult it is in general for young children to mourn their parents, particularly when they could not participate in ritual ceremonies and when there are no physical remains to which they can attach their mourning. And how impossible mourning was in particular for the Jewish children whose parents disappeared in the round-ups.

Firstly, as mentioned before, there was hope that their parents would return, as in rare instances at least one of them did return, and in extremely few cases both. If some did return, why wouldn't *their* parents return someday?

If one's parents were possibly still alive, how could one talk about them as dead? Only by not talking about them could one prevent others from insisting that the parents had died and continue to believe in their eventual return. By not talking about the parents and their possible or real death, none of it became real, because our feeling that something is real requires social validation. That is why in normal mourning we talk so much about the dead person to do both: keep the memory alive, while at the same time giving others with whom we talk the opportunity to convince us that the person mourned is really gone forever. Without such talks, his death remains unreal, and hence can not be mourned.

Secondly, neither in childhood nor at any later time was there any tangible, physical evidence of the parents' death: no corpse to be buried, no grave to be visited. Nor were there any rituals which would have started mourning in a traditional manner, which give it a definite focus and with it facilitates it greatly. Even when all these experiences are available, the work of mourning must extend over a long period before it can be completed, at least up to a certain degree, because traces of it linger on as long as one lives. In some cultures mourning attire is worn for a month, or even a year, as an outer sign that one mourns the dead. In Jewish custom the gravestone is erected only at the anniversary of the death, or of the burial, signifying a ritual ending of the mourning period. For those about whom this book speaks there was neither definite evidence of their parents' or brothers' and sisters' death, nor a definite point in time when mourning could have started, and with it no date at which it could be expected to end.

Friedländer intimates what is involved in mourning long after the event, and why and how people like him were robbed of the chance to engage in a definite period of mourning which, with it, carries the hope of a definite ending. Without such definite points in time, mourning seems impossible to complete, and one is apt to suffer all one's life from its continuation. He writes: "When people leave us... their presence quite naturally anchors itself and survives in the memories of the ones who remain, in the reminiscences and everyday conversations, in the albums one sometimes takes out of the cupboard to show the children, to explain to those who never knew the ones who have departed. From time to time, flowers are put on their graves, and their names are there, engraved in stone... But for me the break was an abrupt one and it cannot become a part of everyday life..."[4]

Jean practically says how having no physical tokens of his parents' lives, nor of their death, makes it impossible to forget it all, and so it is impossible for him to live a normal life. One is tempted to add, because such absence of physical evidence does not permit normal mourning, and through it freeing oneself of grieving permanently. He says, "I often wonder why I don't know how to enjoy life! If I had been able to forget the past completely, perhaps I could have lived 'normally', perhaps I'd have been content with what I have and no longer think about what I don't have any more. I don't have any photos of my parents, I don't have their last letter; I don't even have a grave to visit. Just one document: "Missing... Auschwitz 1943. It's hard."

A remark of Sonia's suggests the impossibility of giving up hope, with the consequence of being eternally disappointed; and the inability to mourn and so free oneself of the continuous presence of the dead in one's mind, until one has some physical evidence. "I realised that my parents' disappearance was permanent thanks to the Klarsfelds' book. When I saw, under the date of 29 April 1944, my parents' names, what a shock! Thirty five years later! It took me thirty five years to admit, finally... You know, I kept on hoping for so long!" Sonia could not help herself carrying on hoping because without mourning we can not really believe that the loved person has died, and without evidence of his death one can not mourn him. The process of mourning alone permits us to accept the death, and with it to give up hope. But although Sonia "knew" that her parents had died long ago, without some tangible evidence, such as the lines published in a book in 1978 mentioning the deportation of her parents, she could not mourn them.

It hardly needs to be mentioned again that, thirdly, there could be no ceremonies which would give the mourning a ritual structure, and with it make mourning possible and direct it toward the acceptance of the loss. Even among not very religious Jews, saying Kaddish for a dead parent is a most important obligation, so much so that in orthodox circles the oldest son was known as the Kaddish, the one who would say the daily mourning prayers after the death of his parents. It was a chance to honour their memory, a most important service one could still render them; being able to do so helped overcome one's feeling of loss.

Important as these factors were in making it impossible for the children to mourn their parents and, after the mourning had been completed, to return to a normal life, they recede into insignificance when compared with the psychological conditions in which the children found themselves on separation of their parents. To mourn means to be in a temporary state of depression because of the loss one has experienced. To be depressed means to have no energy for living and acting. In order to be able to bear the loss of a loved parent without complete collapse, one needs the benefit of the emotional support of family and friends.

But, fourthly, after separation from their parents, if the children were to survive, they could not afford to mourn and with it to fall into a depression. They needed all their vital energy to manage to survive at all. In fact, to be able to adjust to the new conditions, they instantly had to change their way of life, had to become much more energetic and ingenious than they had been ever before. They had to be able to adjust to radically new and different circumstances, to living with people they had not known, under conditions entirely alien to them. And there was nobody around to give them the emotional support they would have needed to be able to permit themselves to feel.

Claudine Rozengard – as her name was then – was extremely lucky in being immediately taken in by foster parents who loved her as if she were their only child, and who could offer her living conditions which, at least in all externals, were as favourable as those she had known before; an incredibly rare exception.

The stories of those whom she interviewed show what incredible difficulties they had to cope with, what radical changes they had to master in order to survive.

Instead of detailing all this once more, I might mention the story of a not yet ten year old Jewish boy whose parents had sent him by pure chance on a short errand. On returning, he saw the house in which he and his family lived surrounded by police. He knew enough to dimly guess what this meant. They had been living for some short time in a small village in the mountains. He immediately turned round, ran out into the open country and hid in a nearby forest. All he had was the address of a person in another village, more than 40 km away. He did not dare to use the railroads, nor had he enough money to pay for a ticket. He avoided the main roads, and hid during the days in the forest. He walked only after dark. Fortunately he had the little food he had been sent out to buy. In two days, or rather nights, he made it to the address given to him. He could not remain there, but was sent on, three times altogether. Later it was the usual story: hiding with farmers, in an institution for feeble-minded children, taking off from there on his own when the other children, although of limited intelligence, nevertheless became aware that nobody visited him and that he received no letters, which made them suspicious, etc.

He barely managed to survive, but he did. To manage it, he needed at all times to muster all his mental and emotional energies. Had he given in to the feelings aroused by seeing his family being taken away, possibly in order to be destroyed, he would never have had the strength to do what was necessary for his survival. He repressed his feelings to be able to do what was necessary to live; that is why he was the only one of a large family to survive.

I have repeatedly referred to the fact that practically all mourning rituals have as their main feature the support which relatives, friends, the community provide for the bereaved, which alone makes full recovery from mourning possible. I also mentioned that children have lost their parents in cataclysmic events without necessarily having suffered permanent damage, although they naturally suffered greatly. This takes me to my fifth and last point. Why were things so different for the Jewish children in France, and in the few other places in Europe where some children managed to survive while their parents were murdered by the Nazis?

Children who are old and intelligent enough to take in, to some degree, their circumstances – and this they do at quite an early age, at least subconsciously – respond to the reaction of the surrounding world to their predicament. Children who, for example, are orphaned by a natural catastrophe know that the rest of the world pities them, wants to help, or at least feels it should help, wants the children to live and not to be adversely affected by their fate. Everybody seems glad that at least they survived. This gives them a feeling of being wanted and supported, and this permits them, as soon as the immediate danger to their lives is over, to engage in the kind of mourning which is possible to them, given their age and maturity. Also efforts are made to find the corpses of their parents, to give them a decent burial, which helps them accept the facts as irreversible, prevents false hopes, helps engage in mourning.

The psychological situation was exactly the opposite in Nazi occupied countries. True, Claudine's foster parents wanted her to survive, did everything possible to assure her survival. All children were helped to survive by some people, otherwise none of them would have survived. And those who helped them did it at great risks to themselves and to their families. But this, while it helped with surviving, was actually the only thing which made survival possible, it did not change the fact that society, the powers which ruled life, the state, the obligation of which is to protect the child's life, were determined to destroy the Jewish children, as it was the state that first robbed them of their parents and then murdered them. It was not unlucky chance that they lost their parents, as it is when children are orphaned because the parents die due to sickness, or a natural catastrophe; it was because their parents were Jews that they were destined to die, parents and children alike.

If parents die through sickness, or from any other cause, there is every reason to assume that the children will be saved; once they survive, they are no longer threatened. But there is no escape from the way one was born; it is an inescapable fate, and even a quite young child somehow knows that. One cannot mourn a parent when one knows one is oneself to die. The purpose of mourning is to free oneself step by step from one's depression about the loss, so that one can go on living. But if one is to die, there is no purpose in mourning others. Only desperation or denial is then psychologically possible.[5]

Claudine Vegh mentions the overwhelming feeling of "permanent danger of death." She does so in a somewhat different context. But I believe this feeling was also motivated by memories of how she had felt while in hiding, and by how she thought the others felt while in hiding, trembling in fear of being discovered and deported into the extermination camps. They knew that while one may hide and be temporarily safe, there is no escape from the way one was born. This is why Claudine Vegh's friend, when asked about his origins, answered that he was "Buchenwaldian."

In denial, be it denial of facts or of feelings, one alienates oneself from them. To use the image evoked by Helen Epstein, one puts these facts and feelings into a carefully and permanently locked box. But try as one may, one can not get rid of this box, and it remains an alien element in one's life which it, nevertheless, controls.

Claudine Vegh concludes, "We, the Jewish children who had lived through the Nazi period, had done all we could to reject that experience as something 'outside ourselves'." But it will not do. We can not externalize the most important facts and experiences of our lives. Try as we may, we can not alienate ourselves from them. If we try, we only alienate ourselves from life. We must accept them as a most important part of ourselves without, however, permitting them to dominate all of our lives. As the stories in this book show, this is exactly what happened; by trying to repress the memories, they only end up by dominating us.

For those who participated in its creation, this book is a most important step in stopping the efforts to deny and to repress, and in beginning the long postponed task of mourning the murdered parents, so that their memory can be laid to rest, and so that finally their children can live a normal life.

I have talked about mourning rather than about the horrible experiences of those whose stories we learn from this book, or the great courage with which they first struggled to survive and with which they later carried the over-heavy burden of their memories. I should have praised the deep sincerity with which they spoke; I should have expressed compassion for their pain. Instead I talked about mourning, because I believe for them mourning was what made their talking with Claudine Vegh significant.

She describes how those she talked with withdrew ever more into themselves as they spoke about the past and the loss of their parents. How they averted their gaze, withdrew to their bedroom or their bed, and cried. As she put it, their talk was "an endless internal monologue." Nevertheless they finally said it aloud and in the presence of a compassionate listener. This is what happens in mourning: one speaks about one's loss, mainly to oneself, but in front of a person willing to share the burden, who understands, who tries to help; this gives one the courage, the strength to mourn.

That those who speak in these pages did indeed begin the all too long delayed process of mourning is suggested by their telling Claudine Vegh on the day following the interview that they felt better, relieved. Maybe we would all be better off if we, too, would engage in mourning the terrible losses we all suffered because of the Nazi murder of the Jews.

[1] This passage is from Part III-1 of Friedländer's book, under the date of October 24, 1977.

[2] Helen Epstein, *Children of the Holocaust*. New York, G. P. Putnam's Sons, 1979.

[3] This passage is in Part II-1 of his book, under the date of September 17, 1977.

[4] This passage is to be found in Friedländer's book, Part II-1, under the date of October 4, 1977.

[5] I found myself in a somewhat parallel situation during my year in Dachau and Buchenwald. One was saddened when a comrade died, but one did not mourn him, for that one was oneself too close to death; and to have given in to the sadness which is part of mourning, would have greatly increased the chance of one's being unable to muster the determination needed to survive. Hence mourning would not have helped one to go on living, but would have impeded it.